Michael Distel

Serenity

Hope

Serenity

Hope

He Calls Me by Name
Book 1

MICHAEL WINSTELL

Serenity Hope
He Calls Me by Name – Book 1
© 2018 by Michael Winstell
www.michaelwinstell.com

All photography by Jennifer Conti
www.jennyvphotography.com
Cover model: Emily Gregory
Photographs used by permission.

Scripture taken from the New King James Version®.
Copyright © 1982 by Thomas Nelson.
Used by permission. All rights reserved.

Set in EB Garamond 12.

This book is a work of fiction.
All people, places, events, and situations are products of the author's imagination or are
used in a satirical or non-literal manner. Any resemblance to persons, living or dead, or
actual events or locales is purely coincidental.

In memory of my grandmother, Marian Carver

I would like to thank:

My editor, Tiffany Cole, for doing another fantastic job. Jennifer Conti (www.jennyvphotography.com) for her amazing photos. Emily Gregory for being a beautiful cover model and a kind friend. Terry Wolf for patiently answering many questions. Sailor and Tucker for being very photogenic and friendly horses. My church family at Community Bible Church, Kennesaw, GA. My family for their support and encouragement.

Finally, and most importantly, the Lord of all creation.

CHAPTER ONE

SUNSET FIRE stretched across the horizon. Serenity Hope MacAlister brushed a strand of chestnut brown hair out of her eyes and rubbed Hillbilly's neck.

"I'll never get tired of this view," she whispered. The horse dipped his head and blew out of his nostrils.

Serenity scanned the hills once more. She was telling Hillbilly the truth: she would always love watching the sun set over the low hills of her family's fifty-acre spread outside of Jonesburg, Texas. It wasn't just the view, either; the air smelled different when twilight came. Softer, sweeter. Serenity inhaled the delicious air and closed her eyes. Somehow, she could still sense all of the vibrant colors – red, orange, pink, purple. These were the moments that she wished could last forever.

Her eyes snapped open and she looked around, embarrassed even though she was alone. Except Hillbilly. But he already knew how kooky she could be sometimes. She rubbed his neck again and leaned close to his ear.

"Ready to head home?"

The horse shook his head.

"Me neither," Serenity said with a grin. The two of them stood on the crest of the hill for a few more minutes, watching the sun sink lower and lower. Just before it kissed the horizon, Serenity heaved a sigh.

"All right, no more dilly–dallying. Mama's going to be mad if I ain't at the table when the cornbread comes out of the oven."

She clicked her tongue and pulled the reins around. As the horse trotted down the hill, she took one last look over her shoulder at the sinking sun.

There's still enough daylight left...

She grabbed the reins with both hands and squeezed her knees tight against the saddle. "C'mon, boy, give it some juice!"

Serenity could sense the horse's delight when she snapped the reins and he broke out into a gallop. The sweet–smelling wind rushed past her face and neck as she crouched low, letting her body sway with the horse's motion. There were only three gentle hills between her and the house but they felt like an ocean. The wind was her companion, whisking her over the water. Her heart pounded and she pulled the reins to the left, circling Hillbilly around the bottom of the last hill before charging up slope to the barn.

Crack Shot and Jasmine, the other horses in the stalls, whinnied and stamped their hooves as Serenity and Hillbilly pulled up just a few yards from the barn door. Serenity hopped down and flung her hair out of her eyes again. She couldn't wipe the big grin off her face even if she wanted to. There were few things in the world she loved as much as galloping across the grassy hills, free as a bird, no worries, no rules...just her, a horse, and the wind.

Of course, there were some things she loved more than galloping across the grassy hills, and most of them were in the house up yonder. Leading Hillbilly into the stall, she unbuckled the cinch, hoisted the saddle off of his back, and removed the bridle.

"Good ride today, boy." She grabbed the brush from the tack room and gave him a quick once-over, then stepped out of the stall and locked the door. Hillbilly poked his head over the top and raised his nose.

Serenity chuckled and gave him one more pet. "Such a mama's boy."

Crack Shot and Jasmine snorted and poked their heads out, too.

"Okay, you big babies," Serenity groaned jokingly as she gave the other horses a few moments of affection. "Sorry that girl kicked you so hard in the ribs today," she said to Crack Shot. "Thanks for not bucking her off."

Crack Shot bared his teeth in a comical smile.

Serenity grabbed the pitchfork from the wall and tossed several clumps of hay into each horse's stall, then checked the water and grain buckets. She would muck the stalls tomorrow morning.

"Okay y'all," she said as she headed to the barn door. "Back at it again tomorrow. Sleep tight."

The three horses whinnied. Serenity blew each one a kiss and closed the barn door. She stepped back and looked up at the wooden structure. There were six stalls inside but only three horses. Daddy said that when he was a boy growing up on this land, his mother always kept the stalls full with her own horses and those she boarded. Fifty acres of grass was more useful back then, too. Serenity knew her father had a sentimental attachment to every inch of this property, but after glancing at those letters from the bank that she had spotted on his desk the other day, she wondered how long he would be able to keep it, since she was the lone horsewoman of the family now.

The evening sky darkened with each passing moment as she took the well-worn dirt path through the grass toward the house, a white two-story farmhouse nestled in a grove of oaks and poplars. Daddy's Ford Expedition was parked next to Mama's brand-new red Mazda sedan. Serenity was still trying to get used to the sight of her driving it, last month's birthday present and her first new car in fifteen years. It had been sad to set the old Toyota Camry out to pasture (out to the junkyard, really) but just like people and horses, every car has its time.

About a hundred yards separated the house from the barn, and it was during these short walks that Serenity found herself slowing down, like a moon caught between two planets. She loved both places and the beautiful creatures inside them. There had been a time when the gravity of the barn seemed to be winning out over the pull from home, but that was before...

Serenity kicked a loose pebble with her boot and looked toward the west. The sun had already gone down, leaving jagged trails of color in the sky. It was strange how clouds always seemed to congregate where the sun went down, like they were being pulled in its wake. The rest of the sky was virtually cloudless, and a couple of stars were visible near the eastern horizon.

She stopped when she passed the one tree that stood on the path between the barn and the house. A stout white oak, most of the leaves now reddish-orange. It was mid-October but the seasons started late in Jonesburg, and in all of Serenity's twenty years – though she could only really remember about fifteen of those years – this tree was always the first on the property to change colors. Sometimes it would be fully turned just a couple of weeks into the season.

In the fading light, Serenity could make out the worn spots on the lowest branch where the rope swing had been. The swing had busted a few years ago when Serenity sat on it after the ropes had endured a harsh winter, and Mama had made Daddy shimmy up there and cut down the broken rope strands because she said it looked like they were lynching folks. Daddy said that wasn't very funny, and Mama said that she wasn't joking. Serenity remembered being paranoid as she held the ladder for him so he could get up there and cut the knots. It was a silly thought, considering how indestructible her father was, but she couldn't help but think of what would happen if he fell the fifteen or so feet from the top of the ladder to the hard ground and broke his neck or hit his head. She couldn't endure another loss like that.

Of course, nothing happened, and Daddy came down with the knife and the frayed pieces of rope. A melancholy moment had passed between them, and then he tossed the rope in the trash and that was that. The tree was also probably happy it didn't have to endure anymore chafing.

Serenity started walking again, but not before her eye caught the jagged "J" carved into the tree trunk. A small, dark line trailed down from the bottom of the letter where the sap had run out. It looked like a tear.

Serenity exhaled slowly and made her way up to the house. She took off her boots on the porch, swatting away a giant beetle that mistook her head for the porch light. When she opened the screen door, she noticed a few holes in the bottom screen that weren't there this morning.

That darn cat...

Beets was always clawing up something around the house. Serenity didn't care for the feline but he was Mama's little angel, no matter how many dead rodents he left on the porch.

Every thought, every emotion evaporated when she opened the kitchen door and smelled that cornbread fresh out of the oven and the seasoned roast in the Crock-Pot. Her mouth began watering instantly.

Patti MacAlister was stirring the boiled veggies. She pointed her wooden spoon at Serenity.

"I saw you and Hillbilly tearing through that grass just now," she said with a huff. "Ain't too smart in the twilight with gopher holes all over the place."

"Yes, Mama." Serenity gave her a kiss. Patti gave her a sidelong smile.

"Felt like a tall drink of freedom, didn't it?"

Serenity smiled back. "Sure did."

Patti sighed and looked up at the wooden kitty cat clock above the stove. It was the same color as Beets. "What I wouldn't give to be young again and ride hard and fast and free as a bird..."

"Ain't nothing stopping you, Mama. You can saddle up any horse any time you want."

"Young lady, you and gravity are still friends. If I get in the saddle and ride like you did, I'd be bouncing north, south, east, and west."

Serenity suppressed a chuckle. *That* would be a sight to see. "Don't matter if no one's watching, Mama."

"That's the problem," Patti said with another wave of her spoon. "When you think no one's watching, you can be sure there is."

"If you say so." Serenity looked at the empty table. "Where's Daddy?"

"Out back in the tool shed. Tell him to get his hide in here before the cornbread gets cold."

"Yes, Mama."

Serenity exited through the back door and almost ran smack into Greg MacAlister coming up the back steps.

"Hey, Daddy."

"Hey, cowgirl." He was a big man with a big grin and a big heart. Serenity gave him a hug.

"Mama said to get your hide in the house before the cornbread gets cold."

"I figured as much." Greg winced as he heaved himself up the last step.

Serenity noticed. "Arthritis acting up again?"

Greg nodded. "Happens every change of season. Going to see the doctor next week, see if they got anything besides pills. I don't want to turn into your Uncle Vernon."

"You're too strong for that, Daddy."

"I hope you're right. Between my arthritis and your mother's thyroid issues, you might have to push around two parents in a wheelchair before too long."

"Just make sure you build a ramp at the front door first."

Greg laughed. "Let's get inside before your mother sends a search party."

****

"Thank You, Lord, for this delicious food prepared by loving hands. Bless it to the nourishment of our bodies, and let us always be grateful for what we have and what we don't. We ask this in Jesus' name, amen."

"Amen."

"Amen."

Serenity had to fight the urge to grab a steaming hunk of meat with her bare hands and tear into it like a savage. She hoped her parents couldn't hear her stomach growling.

Greg heaped a pile of vegetables onto his plate, along with a thick slab of roast beef and a large piece of cornbread.

"So honey," he said as he passed the food to his wife, "how was your day?"

Serenity licked her lips as she watched her mother scoop food onto her own plate.

"Well," Patti began in a tone of voice that indicated the story to follow would not be encouraging, "I stopped by the church to change the decorations on the tables in the fellowship hall, and would you believe that someone had already put out new centerpieces? Without running it by me first?"

Greg's eyebrows rose as he lifted a forkful of roast beef to his mouth. "How about that."

Serenity cleared her throat. "Um, Mama...could you pass the –"

"Sorry, sweetie." Patti handed over the plate and continued her rant. "Everyone knows that I'm in charge of the decorations in the fellowship hall. Have been for the last seven years. I'm no tyrant, and I let plenty of folks put their little spin on things. But to go behind my back like that..."

"Were they nice?"

Patti looked at her husband. "What?"

Greg dabbed his mouth with a napkin. "The centerpieces. Did they look nice?"

Patti's expression seemed to twist in many directions at once. "Well, yes, they were beautiful–"

"So what's the problem?"

"The problem, Gregory, is that *I* wasn't consulted. The chain of command has to be preserved. You don't see me going up to the pulpit on Sunday and cutting Pastor Avery off at the knees, do you?"

"Well, there is that whole 'women be silent in church' thing,"

Greg mumbled.

"What was that?"

"Nothing, dear. Could you pass the salt?"

Patti drew her lips in a line and handed over the salt shaker in the shape of a gnome. "Well, bottom line is, once I find who's taken it upon themselves to play Martha Stewart in my fellowship hall, they're going to get a stern talking-to."

"Mama," Serenity said, her mouth full of food, "it's not *your* fellowship hall."

"Oh, you know what I mean. How's the meat?"

Greg and Serenity both grunted.

"Not too tough?"

Grunts again.

Patti smiled. "Well, at least someone appreciates my contributions." She took a bite of roast beef and nodded to herself. "How about you, dear?"

Greg sipped his water and wiped his mouth. "The new Marlins came in today. Going to take one up to the ridge tomorrow and fire off a few rounds to get a feel for them. Roy Showalter popped in and told me that the council voted on opening up the north bend of the river, which will make the summer tourists happy next year. Lots of smallmouth up thataways so I'll have to stock some new lures."

"Sounds nice, Daddy."

Greg gave Serenity a grateful smile. "I'm hoping so. The

hunting and fishing business always has its ups and downs, but it seems that the Man takes a bigger bite each year in one way or another."

Serenity thought of the letters from the bank but she kept quiet.

"That's why you need to get that website up and going like you talked about," Patti said.

Greg shrugged. "If I could find someone to put it together and not charge me an arm and a leg, I'd be all for it. Then I could sell thirty-aught-sixes to folks in France or Japan."

"I don't think that would work, Daddy."

"A guy can dream, can't he?"

Patti touched her daughter's hand. "How'd it go with the kids today?"

Serenity finished her mouthful of food and said, "Well, that bratty little girl kicked Crack Shot in the ribs again. I could see it in his eyes; he wanted to fling her off into next week."

"You did plenty of kicking yourself when you were just starting out."

"And I got tossed on my rear for it and learned my lesson right quick." Serenity took a deep breath and exhaled slowly. "Well, anyway, aside from that, the kids are loving it. Emily's finally over her fear and lets Jasmine canter around a bit without me holding the lead line. And there are a couple of them that might turn out to be decent riders if they stick with it."

"What do their parents say? They're the ones you really have to sell."

"I don't know. I can tell it's a stretch money–wise for some of them. But the way those kids' eyes light up when they see those horses...I think for some of them, it's the best part of their week. I can tell that a few come from bad home situations, and I'm glad they find some peace with me."

"They find Serenity," Greg said with a wink.

"Oh, you old ham," Patti huffed as she got up to refill her water glass.

"In all seriousness," Greg continued, "I'm proud of you, kiddo. You may not think of yourself this way, but you're an entrepreneur. I wish my mama were still around to see how you've carried on the family tradition. When I turned out to be all pudgy, I could tell she was a little disappointed that I wasn't going to be a rodeo champ. Of course, my daddy was tickled pink when I got into hunting and fishing, but I knew my mama always wanted to keep horses in the family. And now look at you."

Serenity blushed as a shy smile spread across her cheeks. "I'm just a riding instructor, Daddy."

"But do you work for anyone? You got a boss? You clock in and clock out every day? No. *You* did this all by yourself, and you should feel proud."

"Along with plenty of love and support from your family and help from the Good Lord," Patti added as she sat back down.

"I know, Mama. And I thank both of you and the Good Lord."

Greg gave her arm a pat and turned his attention back to his food. Silence settled over the table for a few minutes. Serenity was grateful for the chance to sit and savor her food. Much as she loved her folks, sometimes these moments of quiet were just what she needed.

Patti dabbed her mouth with her napkin and set her cutlery down with a clatter. Serenity instinctively clenched her stomach.

"Have you thought anymore about going to the Harvest Dance next weekend?" Patti asked.

Serenity fought the urge to roll her eyes. "Yes, Mama, I've thought about it."

"...And?"

"And I don't much see the point in going. It's just going to be weird since everyone else will be with their husbands or boyfriends. I'll stick out like a sore thumb."

"You ain't the only single girl in town, sweetie."

"Pretty much."

"And regardless, sticking out like a sore thumb at a dance is a good thing. You should've seen how fast I caught your father's eye at the Spring Fling Do–Si–Do. Right, dear?"

Greg looked up mid–bite. "Oh, yes, of course. Right after I

danced with that handsy redhead and those two Mexican twins, I made a beeline right for your mother."

Patti threw a crumb of cornbread at him. He snickered and kept on eating. Patti pursed her lips and turned back to Serenity.

"Point is, you've got to put yourself out there if you want to meet someone."

"Who says I want to meet someone?"

"Are you telling me that you *don't* want to meet someone?"

Serenity hesitated, then shrugged. "Well, no...but it don't mean I *do* want to meet someone either. At least not right now."

Patti touched her hand. Serenity was starting to feel like a velvet pillow with all the touching going on.

"Sweetie," her mother said, "I don't want to be the kind of mother you see in the movies who ruins her daughter's life by pressuring her into a relationship. But I also don't want you to sit at home waiting for Prince Charming."

"I *know,* Mama. And I ain't just sitting at home waiting for Prince Charming."

"I know you're not, sweetie. But you're young, you're beautiful – not that that's a surprise," she added with an exaggerated flip of her hair, eliciting a whistle from Greg, "and most of all, you have a beautiful heart full of love for the Lord and kids and horses, and any man would be the luckiest fool in God's green earth to have his hand in yours."

"Amen," Greg added.

Serenity blushed again. "Now both of you stop it." She looked at the ceiling and sighed. "All right Mama, I'll go to the stupid dance, but I ain't looking to hitch my wagon to anyone for a good long while. You've got to leave me be."

"Sweetheart," Patti said in a hushed voice as she leaned in close, "no mother can ever leave her children be."

"Ain't that the truth," Greg mumbled to his plate.

"You say something, dear?"

"Nope."

Serenity looked at both of them and shook her head. Maybe finding a handsome fellow wouldn't be such a bad idea; the alternative was spending the rest of her life with Lucy and Desi here.

Who was she kidding? She knew practically every guy in town, most of whom she had gone to school with and already knew more about than she needed to. All the good ones were either married or had moved on to bigger and brighter places or both. Maybe a girl like her could find freedom and happiness in the windswept plains but if a guy stayed here, it was because he was stuck. More than a few of her former classmates were deep in the clutches of alcohol or meth, and they were likely going to be the ones at the dance hoping for an easy score. Trouble was, there were plenty of other girls around who would be happy to get caught for all the wrong reasons, and in their eyes, Serenity would be just another fish in the river.

But she promised her Mama, and she did like to dance. At least she used to... And who knows, maybe she'd just have a nice evening with friends. Cassie and Kelly said they were going, and they were pretty much the only decent girls left in town who were still "unhitched," as it were. Besides, Serenity was still friends with several guys in town, and maybe their wives or girlfriends wouldn't begrudge her one little dance...

Yeah, right. *"Yes, that's my husband out there dancing with the twenty-year-old."* She knew she wouldn't abide it if she were in their shoes. Why did simple things in life have to be so doggone complicated sometimes?

She looked at her parents, who were now talking about the church decorations again. She smiled to herself.

Lucy and Desi. Got to love 'em.

CHAPTER TWO

SERENITY YAWNED as she walked down the dark hallway to her room. She passed the rows of pictures on the walls, catching Josh's eye as he stared at her from his junior prom picture. He looked like he was trying his hardest not to break out in a goofy smile, probably because he wanted to impress the girl in the picture with him.

Just a few feet past the picture was the door to his room. Serenity paused for a moment and peeked inside. Moonlight streamed in through the window and fell upon the bed in bars of white–blue light. Everything in the room was clean and in its place, which was never how the room actually looked when Josh had slept in it. Mama cleaned it a couple of times a month, even though hardly any dust accumulated on the furniture. It was her memorial to him, and Serenity thought it was sweet. Sadness pricked at her heart as she looked around the room, at the trophies and posters and books and various knick–knacks. She could still feel him, his mischievous laugh, his unquenchable curiosity.

Miss you, bro.

She closed the door and went to her room. After changing into her pajamas and brushing her teeth, she climbed into bed and grabbed her phone from the nightstand. She scrolled through social media for a little while but nothing caught her interest. Heaving a weary sigh, Serenity looked up from her phone and stared at the full moon for a few moments, marveling at how bright it was despite having no light of its own. She remembered reading something about that in a devotional a while back, how believers in Christ are like the moon, merely reflecting God's light, but even that reflection can be incredibly brilliant. The light of the moon is still nothing compared to the sun, just as the light in a Christian's heart is nothing compared to the light of God's love, but it comes from the same source and when the sun cannot be seen, the moon is there to give comfort. Serenity felt that way with some of her kids. There were two in particular, a boy and a girl, both about twelve, and she knew they were having serious issues at home. The problem was, they were bringing those issues to riding class. The horses and fresh air were good for them but the anger and hurt that was knotted up inside them sometimes manifested itself as rebellion or rudeness. It wasn't anything too serious and Serenity knew she was just their riding instructor and not their counselor or therapist, but it still bothered her in her heart. She wanted all of her kids to be happy and have the best experience they could, even just for a couple hours a week. In the end, though, Serenity knew it wasn't up to her. Last Sunday, Pastor Avery had talked about keeping our impact on others in the right perspective. *We* don't save anyone; *we* don't lead anyone to Christ; *we* don't change other people's lives. God does that through us, but He's the one who makes it happen, and recognizing His timing is just as important as recognizing His power.

Serenity took a deep breath and prayed a quick, silent prayer. *Lord, use me to reach those that You want me to reach, and to let You take care of the rest.*

In the deep, dark sky, the moon seemed to glow just a little brighter.

She picked up her phone and hitched the blanket up to her chin. She wasn't nearly as active on social media as most of her peers, but she followed many people who also loved horses and she liked seeing their pictures and videos. Her thumb bobbed up and down as she scrolled through Instagram, and her eyelids started feeling heavy. She was about to set the phone on the nightstand when she stopped and stared.

It was a photo of Cal Brookfield, her ex-boyfriend, on the beach with Vanessa Timms. Clearwater, Florida, according to the location tag. He was the one taking the selfie, his shirtless torso tanned and muscular, his biceps flexed. Vanessa was wearing an

American flag bikini, pressing her body against his, twisting in a seductive pose and kissing the camera.

Serenity stared at the picture for several minutes, studying every detail. She had never been to the beach, and Cal, a Florida native, had promised that he would take her one day. Of course, that was before she found out he was sleeping with Vanessa since Serenity wouldn't go beyond kissing. This was going on while all three of them were in the Young Singles' Bible study at church. That had been more than a year ago. Serenity knew he and Vanessa had moved to Florida together and had seen several of their pictures online, but something about this picture really twisted the knife in her back.

They looked so happy. And so hot. And so free.

That should've been me...

Serenity's cheeks flushed and she felt equally jealous and embarrassed. She dropped the phone on the blanket and stared at the dark wall at the foot of the bed.

She knew she had never truly loved Cal. She had loved the *idea* of Cal – a handsome, smooth-talking beach boy bringing his easygoing sunshine to the plains of Texas. And after all of the turmoil she had gone through the year before she met him, she had needed someone to latch onto.

Well, it was her fault for giving him her heart in the first place. You'd think she'd have learned her lesson about roguish bad boys after all that drama with Rick Stevens. She was glad Rick wasn't on social media, at least as far as she knew.

Where is Rick? Was he still in Afghanistan? Was he even still in the service? A lot had happened in those years after Josh's death. She'd broken up with Rick, met Cal, and broke up with him, too. She wondered what she would say to Rick if she suddenly saw him again out of the blue. Would she even *want* to say anything to him?

She glanced down at her phone and smirked. Cal wasn't that special, anyway. He was just her rebound after Rick. Let him frolic on the beach with Vanessa, that spoiled princess.

Serenity stewed for a couple of minutes, then keyed in the website address for Aunt Lillian's horse training school in Nebraska. Aunt Lillian wasn't really her aunt, just her mother's good friend. As far as Serenity could remember, she had always been "Aunt" Lillian. But the important thing was that Lillian loved horses and had a pretty sweet school up near Lincoln. She had asked on several occasions if Serenity would like an apprenticeship up there with her, which would most likely turn into a full-time job, which would also open up many doors, academically and professionally. When she was getting ready to graduate from high school, Serenity had all but made up her mind to go, even though it would mean moving away from her family and friends. Something about it just felt right.

All of that was before Josh died and her world got turned upside-down. Now Lincoln, Nebraska might as well be on the moon shining in her window. She tossed the phone on the nightstand and burrowed into the blanket. Why had she even looked at that thing? First Cal, and now digging up old dreams. If there was one thing the internet was good for, it was stirring up discontentment.

Serenity squeezed her eyes shut, even though her mind was wide awake and her heart ached.

My name is Serenity...so why can't I ever find peace?

****

Serenity held the reins tight and shielded her eyes from the sun as she looked up at the girl on the horse.

"See, Heather? You just have to trust him. He's happy to give you a ride. He ain't looking to buck you off or nothing."

Heather smiled. She was eleven years old, and this was only her second lesson. Her first class a few days ago didn't go so well; she wouldn't even get on the horse. It took Serenity nearly all of the hour and a half lesson time to convince Heather it was okay to touch the animal. Serenity figured from her parents' accents that they were city folk from somewhere on the West Coast and Heather obviously had no prior experience with horses, or perhaps a bad experience. Serenity didn't want to pry, and Heather wasn't her first reluctant student. In the spring, there had been a boy who flat—out refused to get on the horse for three weeks. Lord knows why his parents kept spending their money to keep him under Serenity's tutelage, but little by little, she helped him overcome his fear. His parents split up that summer and he moved away with his mom but she was glad she was able to bring him some joy.

It seemed like Heather's home and family situation was fine, but they were new in town, only a few months, and that had to be hard on a kid, especially coming to a place like Jonesburg. Serenity remembered Daddy telling her that moving out to the country is easier the older you are, and unless you're born in it, country life generally doesn't set well with younger folks. She could hardly fathom growing up in a crowded, smog-choked city, or even those factory-made suburbs where if you kicked a rock in any direction, you'd hit a neighbor's house. No, Serenity needed the wide horizon and open plains. She didn't mind going into town now and then but her heart was out here.

And maybe one day, Heather's heart would be out here, too. Serenity gave the girl a smile as she led Hillbilly around the arena with Heather perched on his back.

"Hold that horn tight," she said, "and keep your feet firm in those stirrups. Just relax your body and let yourself rock with the horse's stride. Think of the horse like one of them big medicine balls – you ever sat on one of those?"

Heather nodded.

"Hillbilly here ain't that squishy but the idea is the same.

Riding on a horse ain't like riding in a car, all smooth and boring. With a horse, you walk and sway at the same time. Makes it more fun."

"Miss Serenity?"

"Yeah, sweetie?"

"Will he bolt if you let go of the strings?"

"The reins?"

"Yeah."

"No, sweetie. I told you before, he's pleased as punch to have such a pretty little lady on his back. He's probably tired of carrying me around."

"But you're real pretty too, Miss Serenity."

"Well, thank you, darling. You're sweet. And even if that's true, Hillbilly's happy to tote around another pretty gal. There ain't a thing in the world that would make him bolt or buck you off."

"You sure?"

"'Course I'm sure. You want to try?"

"I'm scared."

"Don't be. I'll stand right here. If he even twitches, I'll grab the reins. He always listens to his mama."

Heather tightened her fingers around the saddle horn and bit her bottom lip. "Okay," she said cautiously. "Don't let him kick me off."

"You got nothing to worry about, sweetie."

Before Heather could change her mind, Serenity swung the reins over the horse's head. Heather's eyes went wide for a moment. Hillbilly just stood there, his tail swishing away a fly. Heather looked down at him, as if she were afraid of making eye contact. Serenity let ten seconds elapse.

"See? He's as gentle as a kitten."

She stroked his face and gave him a kiss before looking up at Heather.

"How do you feel?"

"Fine, I guess. I wish I knew what he's thinking right now."

"Probably thinking about the carrots I got in my pocket." She pulled one out and fed it to the horse. "Good boy. And I'm proud of you, Heather. You're a brave girl."

Heather beamed.

"You want to try something even more brave? I know you can handle it."

"Sure."

Serenity could see the confidence in the girl's face. Confidence is the key to learning new skills.

She picked up the reins that were draped on the back of Hillbilly's neck and offered them to the girl. "I'm going to give you the reins. That way, Hillbilly knows you're in control. We're just going to walk along the fence like we've been doing. I'll be right alongside you just like this. But you'll be in control. How does that sound?"

Heather took the reins, holding them gingerly in front of her. "I...I guess so."

"You're brave, remember? And I'll be right here next to you. Ready?"

Heather nodded.

"Give them a little flick."

With a nervous expression, Heather gave the reins a timid snap and Hillbilly began walking forward. Serenity fell in step alongside the horse, a couple of feet back so that she wouldn't be in his field of vision, but Heather didn't know that.

She looked up at the girl in the saddle. "How does that feel?"

Heather was grinning like a child at Christmas. "It feels awesome! I'm making him walk!"

"You sure are. Horses are like people – they don't like being forced to do something but they respond to leadership. You lead, and the horse will follow."

"This is so cool!"

Serenity's heart swelled with happiness as she walked with the horse and his rider along the perimeter of the arena. Since starting her riding classes two years ago, she had helped more than a dozen kids who were totally fearful of horses become enthusiastic riders, and that's not counting the dozens more who already had riding experience and were looking to go to the next level. Those kids were great too, but it was kids like Heather that really brought her the most joy. Serenity loved being able to open their eyes and their hearts to an amazing world and hopefully to the realization that horses were more than just animals – they were friends, and sometimes, even family.

Hillbilly started picking up speed and a look of worry crossed Heather's face.

"Um, Miss Serenity..."

Serenity clamped her mouth shut to keep from giggling. "Just pull back on the reins a bit. Nice and easy."

Heather gave the reins a hard yank, and for a moment, Serenity was worried that Hillbilly might rear back and startle his rider. But he was a wise horse and knew how to handle these young whippersnappers, and he just slowed his gait a bit, settling back into a nice, meandering walk.

"I did it!" Heather exclaimed.

"You sure did. I told you, he wants to listen to you. Just like driving a car...well, for you, like riding a bike. Where you lead, he'll follow."

She let the horse take the girl around the arena a few more times before stepping forward and hushing him to a halt.

"That was so fun," Heather said as Serenity helped her down.

"Were you scared?"

Heather shook her head. "A little at first, but then I started to...sort of..."

"Trust him?"

"Yeah. I trusted him. And I felt safe."

"And you should. The last rider Hillbilly tossed in the dirt was this ornery gal many years ago who didn't know the first thing about riding."

Heather blinked, then grinned. "It was you!"

Serenity snapped the brim of her hat. "Yep. I learned my lesson. Plus, Hillbilly's a bit older and wiser now. He knows not to make his mama angry."

She rubbed the horse's nose and fed him another carrot. "Let's walk him back home and wait for your folks," she said to Heather.

The three of them started heading back to the barn. The sun was high and the weather was a few degrees warmer than yesterday, though Serenity could feel the nip of autumn in the breeze.

"How's school going?" she asked.

Heather shrugged. "All right, I guess."

"You making any friends?"

Heather shrugged again.

"Well, what's that mean?"

"I suppose. No one's mean to me or nothing, but..."

"But what?"

"But I just feel sort of different from everybody."

"Well, everybody's different from everybody."

"I feel *more* different."

"Because you ain't from around here?"

"I guess. I like it here; I like you and the horses, and my parents like it, too. But I didn't grow up on a farm or up on a mountain. I grew up in a big neighborhood outside of Sacramento. And I feel like that's what everyone sees when they look at me."

"What's wrong with growing up in a neighborhood outside of Sacramento?"

"Nothing. But I feel like other people think there is something wrong with it."

Serenity brought Hillbilly to a halt and looked at Heather.

"Listen, I'm just your horse riding teacher, and I ain't never lived in a suburban McMansion, but I was your age not too long ago, just a kid trying to make it through the crazy world of middle school. I remember worrying what people thought of me; to tell you the truth, I still do. I don't think that ever goes away, especially for us girls. But that's just a fact of life. The kids at school may or may not be judging you because of where you came from, but they're just as worried as you are. Maybe they ain't worried about where they came from, but they're worried about their hair, their clothes, their weight, their accent, their cheerleading moves, their family's reputation. Honestly, you have the advantage of being new in town. Those other kids, everyone knows all about them and their secrets and screw-ups.

"Bottom line, though, is that nobody is better than you because of where you come from. Don't even matter who is prettier or who is more popular or who has a boyfriend yet. The only thing that makes you better or worse than someone is how you treat other people. If you always treat other people with kindness and respect, ain't no way anyone could be better than you, because that's the top of the ladder."

Heather's mouth hung open. "Wow. I wish my mom was wise like you."

"What do you mean?"

"I told her what I told you and she just said, 'It's all in your head, Heather. Don't imagine yourself to be a victim.'"

"Well, that's good advice, too. It's easy to think that people are thinking something when they really ain't." She paused, then added, "But when it comes to school, people are probably thinking what you're thinking they're thinking."

Heather chuckled. "Well, thanks, Miss Serenity. I'll try not to worry too much."

"Atta girl." She tugged on Hillbilly's reins and they continued down the path.

"Miss Serenity?"

"Yes?"

"Will you come to my school and talk to my class? I want them to see what a cool teacher I have."

"You know what? I think I might just do that. It'd be good for business, too."

"And bring Hillbilly."

Serenity laughed. "Oh, of course!"

CHAPTER THREE

SERENITY KEPT a firm grip on the steering wheel with her right hand as she guided the Ford F–250 down the narrow dirt road. With her left hand, she held her phone to her ear.

"Mama?" she said when the ringing stopped. "Can you hear me all right?"

"Sure, sweetie. What's wrong?"

"Nothing, Mama. I'm just heading into town to get some things."

"What kind of things?"

"Just some personals, get my Ariats resoled, pick up a new halter for Jasmine. You want me to get anything for the house? We all right on toilet paper?"

"I made that Costco run last week, remember? We are well–stocked on everything we need and plenty of things we don't."

"You need me to pick up your medicine?"

"Not yet. Still good for now."

"Okay. Where are you?"

"Helping Rebekah bake a cake for her niece's wedding. I'll be back in time to get dinner going."

"I'll be home then so I'll help too."

"Thanks, hon. Oops, got to go. Frosting emergency. Bye, sweetie."

"Bye Ma – "

The call ended and Serenity tossed the phone onto the passenger seat. *Bless her heart.* If there was cooking to be done, you can bet that Mama would be involved in some capacity. And with the way Daddy ate, Serenity could see why he fell head over heels for her right off the bat. *Maybe I should study her techniques...*

She blew her hair out of her eyes. She could already cook a decent meal. And so what if she learned how to make buttermilk biscuits or squash casserole like Mama? How would that help her find someone? Was she going set up a table by the side of the road and hope that an eligible bachelor drove by?

Just be content, girl. God will bring the right guy your way when it's the right time.

Serenity knew it in her head but she wasn't so sure in her heart, especially after the ditches she'd already crashed into on the road of love. Why was there so much pressure on girls? What was so wrong with being single, anyway? People acted like any halfway–attractive girl without a man's arm around her was some kind of leper or lunatic. Why couldn't she just ride horses every day for the rest of her life?

Would that really make you happy? Just you and your horses forever?

Serenity rubbed the steering wheel.

No.

There wasn't anything wrong about wanting love, either. Everyone does, right? Serenity glanced at her reflection in the rearview mirror. She knew she was pretty. Maybe not beautiful, but she knew she could dazzle with some makeup and a sassy hairdo. It wasn't hard for her to catch men's eyes. Heck, she could feel them watching her wherever she went, even in church. Even some of the married guys.

Finding a man wasn't a problem. The problem was finding the *right* man. Casual dating and hookups were a waste of time and potentially dangerous, not to mention against the Bible. There was plenty of immorality around but she wasn't going to let herself get caught up in it. Too bad not many guys shared the same feelings...

Her truck reached the end of the dirt driveway and Serenity turned right at the rusty old mailbox onto Route 146, the two-lane blacktop road that would take her into town. It was an eight minute drive, and the road was more or less straight the whole way.

Driving is so boring compared to horseback riding. Serenity flicked on the radio. The first station was on a commercial so she switched over to the next one. She pretty much only listened to country and gospel music, and there were plenty of stations around here for both. She found a station playing country classics from the '70s and '80s and she sped down the road to Ricky Skaggs singing about being just a country boy at heart.

The road into town might have been boring compared to the windswept freedom of riding a horse, but that didn't mean it had to be a boring ride. Serenity rolled down the window and let her hair blow around her face as she took in the broad Texas sky anchored by the gentle swell of lush green hills and sprawling fields. There were places all over the world where people would say, "This is God's country," but here, Serenity really felt it was true. There were problems everywhere, but that didn't stop the sun from shining or the grass from growing or the wind from blowing. No economic troubles or social strife or class struggles or religious disagreements could diminish the beauty of what she was looking at. And she knew, deep in her heart, that this would always be home.

Her first stop was at C.C. Ray's Feed 'n Steed on the outskirts of town. She pulled into the parking lot and hopped out of the truck, taking a moment to sniff the air.

Manure. That meant Art Calhoun was around. She looked to her left and sure enough, there was his battered 1976 Datsun pickup, the bed piled high with rich, dark manure. It stank to high heaven but that manure enriched Art's plot of "nuclear" hot peppers, as he called them, and his hot sauces were a staple in every restaurant and most kitchens in the county.

The man himself was coming out of the store as Serenity was heading in. He was a lanky old fellow who looked mean and crotchety but he was one of the most cheerful people in town. He was the fiddler at church, and he was also the biggest fan of Patti's homemade bread who didn't have the last name of MacAlister. Patti always bragged about how much Art loved her bread, as if her own family's enthusiastic appetite wasn't convincing enough.

"Howdy, little missy," he said as he held the door open for her.

"Howdy, Mr. Calhoun."

"How're your folks doin'?"

"They're fine. Daddy's at the store and Mama's helping a friend bake a cake."

"Tell her I've got a basketful of ripe zucchinis that I'll gladly trade for a few loaves of her rye bread."

"She'll be happy to hear it."

Just as she stepped into the store, Art spoke up again.

"One more thing, sweetheart."

"Yes?"

Art shifted his feet. "Well, um, my boy Henry, he, uh, well, he wanted me to ask you, you know in case I saw you around town, he wanted me to ask you if you had a mind to be goin' to the Harvest Dance this Saturday."

Serenity cocked her hips and narrowed her eyes. "I might have a mind to. Is Henry going?"

"Well, he certainly would be more inclined if he knew you'd be there. I know you know he's always been sweet on you, and I know he ain't got a snowball's chance in...he ain't got no chance with you or any girl for that matter, and he don't get out much to social events like this, and...well, I just want to say that a friendly smile and a kind word would go a long way with him."

Serenity offered him a warm smile. "You're very sweet, Mr. Calhoun. I'm touched how much you care for that boy, especially with his mama gone. And I'd be happy to give him a kind word and a smile. Maybe even a dance if the song calls to my feet."

Art beamed. "That'd be just swell, Miss Serenity. I hope I don't make you uncomfortable, and I ain't trying to insinuate nothin'. I'm just trying to give that boy any slice of happiness I can. It's been hard with Ellie gone."

"You're doing fine, Mr. Calhoun. And I'm sure Henry appreciates it."

"Thank you, sweetheart. I'm sorry to keep you. I've got to get back to the farm. I'm sure you smelled my manure stinkin' up the place."

"Well, now that you mention it..."

They both chuckled, and Art tipped his hat.

"So long, Miss Serenity. Tell your mama I'll have that zucchini waiting for her at church on Sunday."

"You bet."

Art went to his truck and Serenity stepped inside the store. A dozen smells drifted into her nostrils – sawdust, leather, grass seed, fertilizer, corn meal, and more. It was C.C. Ray's, a genuine north Texas institution. C.C. said that his great–great–granddaddy had a feed store on this very spot when Texas was still part of Mexico.

C.C. looked up from his papers spread out on the counter. "Howdy there, Miss Serenity," he called out across the store.

Serenity walked over to him and grinned. "Howdy yourself, C.C."

C.C. scribbled his signature and organized the papers. "Was Art talking your ear off?"

"No more than usual."

"I get the feeling he's lonely sometimes with Ellie gone and all. He's got Henry, of course, but with that boy's condition, he ain't exactly the sit–on–the–porch–and–converse type."

"Maybe so. But it's good to see him out and about."

"And stinkin' up my parking lot."

Serenity nodded. "It's all a matter of perception." She dropped the halter on the counter. "Jasmine's due for a new one."

C.C. picked it up and held it close to his pudgy, bearded face. "Yep, this one's about finished. One good snap and it will just fall right to pieces."

"Don't want that to happen with a six-year-old on her back."

"How are the lessons going?" C.C. asked as he eased his bulky body through a gap in the counter and led her toward the right side of the store. "From what I hear, you're keeping pretty busy."

"Four days a week, two or three kids a day."

"Ain't that somethin'. It's nice to see young folks like yourself with that entrepreneurial spirit. Your grandmama would've been proud of you."

Serenity shrugged, though the compliment warmed her heart. "Just made sense, I guess. Go with what you know."

"Amen, little sister. That's why that Asian-Mexican – what did they call it? – 'fusion' restaurant over on Pikes Road closed down after less than a year in business. What's wrong with barbecue? This is Texas, not San Francisco. Fusion is for nuke-yoo-ler reactors."

Serenity had to laugh. "I actually ate there once. The food was pretty decent. A little expensive but still nice."

C.C. snorted. "When I want Mexican, I eat at Los Reyos. When I want Asian, I eat at Panda Garden. I don't want them two gettin' together and havin' a baby."

Serenity burst out in a laugh that echoed across the store. She clamped her hand over her mouth and blushed with embarrassment. C.C. looked at her with a strange expression, and she waved her hand in front of her mouth like she was swatting gnats.

"Sorry," she stammered, "but that's the funniest thing I've

heard all week."

C.C. gave her a sidelong grin. "My wife always tells me I'm a comedian."

He stopped in front of a wall display where several halters hung on hooks. "You want the same one or something that'll hold together a bit longer?"

Serenity looked over the selection and pointed. "Can I take a look at that one?"

"You sure can." C.C. brought it down and handed it to her. Serenity held the halter gingerly, feeling the leather and examining the craftsmanship of the knots.

"How much?" she asked.

"For you, I'll give you the C.C. discount and knock off ten percent."

"You don't have to do that."

"I know. But I just did."

"Thanks," Serenity said with a smile. "Ring 'er up."

A few minutes later, she was on her way to Marlow's General Store right in the heart of downtown. There was a Shop–Rite a few minutes closer but Serenity loved these little Mom–and–Pop stores. Sometimes she felt like an old timer in a young person's body. Besides, Marlow's was next door to Quik Fiks Shoe Repair and she needed to get new soles for her favorite pair of Ariat boots, the ones with the angel wings design stitched into the leather. They had been a Christmas present from her grandfather before he died three years ago, and she was going to wear them until her toes were poking out.

After she dropped off her boots, she went over to Marlow's.

"Howdy, Miss Nancy," she said as she picked up a basket.

A smiling woman with horn–rimmed glasses and a large perm of gleaming white hair looked up from her catalog. "Well hello, Serenity! Haven't seen you in a spell."

"The kids and Mama keep me busy."

"I'm sure they do. Help you find something?"

"Just here for my lady things. Might grab me a candy bar if it strikes my fancy."

"I can already tell that it does."

Serenity went searching down the aisles. She found her items quickly, then started browsing just to kill some time. As she scanned the shelves of cookware, cutlery, small appliances, and home decor, she let her imagination drift and roam. What kind of house would she have one day? She couldn't imagine living in a cramped apartment in a big city, but would she decorate like her mama, country cottage/farmhouse style? Would she have shiny steel appliances and sleek leather furniture? Would she have Navajo blankets tossed over the back of wood–framed sofas?

It was exciting to let her mind wander like this, but she also felt a little guilty. She loved her folks and living with them was a joy. Was it wrong to fantasize about having her own place, though? Don't be silly, she told herself. Every girl grows up and becomes the queen of her own home. It doesn't mean she isn't appreciative of her parents or hates living with them. It's just nature's way, and more importantly, God's way. A man and a woman are supposed to find their own path out of their parents' shadow.

Plus, Serenity knew it really didn't matter what kind of home you lived in. What mattered was *whom* you shared your home with. Serenity didn't watch those reality TV shows about Hollywood housewife divas, but she knew that expensive plates and vaulted living room ceilings can't keep a woman happy, no matter what the magazines and commercials say. A handsome, hardworking man who loved the Lord could make the smallest cabin feel like a fairy tale castle.

At least that's what Serenity believed. And she hoped to heaven that it was true.

She blinked and realized that she was in the aisle with all of the ribbons and bows and pretty things that sparkled and glittered. The colors were so beautiful – reds, purples, pinks, whites, lavenders, blues...When was the last time she had worn a ribbon in her hair? She reached up and touched her shoulder–length hair, twisting her fingers in the wavy curls. She would sometimes braid her hair on both sides or wear it in a ponytail, though she would always just use an elastic hair band for that. There was a box in her closet with bows and ribbons that she had worn as a child, but as she grew up, her attention drifted toward flattering jeans and pretty boots and hats.

Her fingers drifted through the dangling ribbons. The thin strands of fabric glided through her fingers like water. The Harvest Dance was on Saturday, just a couple of days away. She wasn't going with anyone special and she didn't have any illusions about meeting anyone special, but that didn't mean she couldn't look special. Why not sprinkle on a little extra pretty?

She hoisted her basket onto the checkout counter, grabbing a Three Musketeers candy bar from the rack and throwing it in at the last minute. Miss Nancy's eyebrows rose when she saw the sky blue ribbon tucked in among the other items.

"Well ain't that a pretty color," she said as the scanner beeped with rhythmic precision. "I can't recall seeing you wear a ribbon in your hair in a while, 'least not since you was a wee little thing and your mama used to dress you up like Laura Ingalls Wilder."

Serenity felt her cheeks grow warm. "Gee, Miss Nancy, I felt so embarrassed wearing those dresses. I felt like I was in a wagon train reenactment or something."

"You was as cute as a button and I won't hear otherwise. Feeling a bit sentimental for those days?"

"No, just... It's nice to feel pretty sometimes."

"Sweetheart, you're pretty all the time." She smiled when Serenity blushed again. "But I completely understand. You should've seen Frank's eyes light up when I would get a new dress. Of course in those days, that weren't more than once or twice a year, which helped to make it a special occasion. But I tell you, there ain't too many feelings like watching your man's eyes shine when he sees you wearing something new. Speaking of which, why isn't some handsome young fellow showing you off around town? You're one of the prettiest girls around. I'll bet the boys are tripping over themselves to ask you out. Is that what the ribbon is for? Already got a handsome fellow in mind?"

Serenity pursed her lips and gave Miss Nancy a glare. "You sound like my mama."

"I'll take that as a compliment," Miss Nancy declared with a haughty expression. "That'll be $19.76. Well how about that? That's the year our oldest son George was born."

"How about that." Serenity paid and took her bags. "See you next time, Miss Nancy."

"Take care, sweetheart," Miss Nancy called after her. "I hope the ribbon does the trick."

Serenity groaned silently as she tossed the bags onto the passenger seat of the pickup. She knew what was going to happen – Miss Nancy would tell all of her lady friends that Serenity had bought a ribbon at her store and that meant she had her eye on someone, and the story would snowball until she was practically engaged. And then Mama would find out and demand to know why she hadn't been told sooner, and Serenity would have to deflate the balloon before it popped. Gossip had a way of sprouting like weeds in a small town like this.

Not that she could blame them, though. There weren't too many girls her age who were still single around town, and most of those that were either had babies on their hips or were bouncing around like a pinball from one guy to the next. It was sweet of everyone to want to see her in a happy relationship, but it was also annoying. It was the same everywhere she went: *"You're too pretty not to be with someone."* As if she were wasting her youth and beauty by not being attached to a man.

Serenity gripped the steering wheel and took a deep, calming breath. These were good people and they meant well. And she wasn't a special case; every one of them probably was the object of small-town gossip at one time or another. It's just human nature – people are curious and they like to talk. And talk and talk and talk.

As she turned the key to start the truck, Serenity glanced over at the bag on the passenger seat. The sky blue ribbon peeked out from beneath the plastic.

It's just a ribbon, and it's just a dance.

If other people wanted to make a big deal, then fine. Social pressure and prying eyes were just facts of life. They couldn't ruin her fun if she didn't let them.

Serenity tossed her hair over her shoulder as she reversed out of the parking lot and drove out to the road. There was one place

where she wouldn't run into any of this nonsense: Mr. Mac's
Hunting and Fishing Supplies.

CHAPTER FOUR

"HI, DADDY."

Greg looked over his customer's shoulder and smiled. "Hi, darling."

Serenity waited until the customer was finished before approaching the counter and giving her father a peck on the cheek.

"What brings you by?" Greg asked as he flipped through some pages on a clipboard.

"Nothing special," Serenity said with a shrug. She scanned the shop, checking to see if anything was new since last week. Same guns on the wall, same fishing poles on their stands, same shelves of lures and hooks and deer calls and camo vests, same taxidermied animals mounted on plaques, most of them caught or killed by Greg himself. The exception was the six-pointer above the door. That was Serenity's first and only kill, when she was eleven years old. She didn't feel bad about it, and she was glad for the experience, but hunting just wasn't her thing, especially after she discovered horse-riding the very next summer.

"How's business?" she asked, sliding around the counter corner and hopping up on the barstool Daddy kept behind the register. Her voice carried a hint of caution.

"Can't complain," Greg answered, heading over to the ammo cage to take inventory. "Deer season starts in a couple of weeks and that always brings the city folks in. Got to make sure I'm all stocked up on the right kind of hardware." He peeked at her over his glasses. "Your mama send you over to check on me or something?"

"No," Serenity said with a sly grin as she slid off the barstool. "I came by to give you this."

She pulled a candy bar out of her back pocket and handed it to him. Greg's face lit up. "Woo–hoo, Three Musketeers! King size, too!"

He looked at her with a grave expression.

"Don't tell your mama about this."

"Cross my heart."

Greg ripped open the wrapper and took a bite. He looked like he was about to faint with happiness.

"You win Daughter of the Month," he mumbled with his mouth full. "I love your mother's cooking but she knows I got a sweet tooth and she has my taste buds on lockdown. Thanks for being my dealer."

"Anytime," Serenity chuckled. She ran her hand over the

rough–hewn counter. "Daddy, can I ask you something?"

"Of course, darling."

Serenity licked her lips and furrowed her brow as she chose her words. "Are you–"

The bell over the door chimed and three men in camouflage coveralls walked into the store.

"Help you, gentlemen?" Greg called out.

"Sure can," one of them said.

Greg gave Serenity's arm a squeeze as he headed toward the group. "We'll talk at dinner, okay sweetheart?"

"Sure," Serenity said, forcing a smile to the surface. "Oh, do you think you could pick up my boots from Quik Fiks after you close up?"

"You bet."

"Thanks. See you at home."

Greg was already chatting with his customers as Serenity left the store. She got in the truck and turned over the engine, but she didn't drive off right away. Something felt unquiet in her soul.

She knew what she needed.

She needed to pray.

And she needed to ride.

****

Serenity's heart pounded along with Jasmine's hoofbeats. She let her feet relax in the stirrups and squeezed the saddle with her thighs, letting her body sway with the galloping motion.

The cool afternoon breeze stroked its gentle fingers across her face and blew her hair back, the strands whipping around the brim of her hat. A sea of grass extended as far as she could see, broken only by a small fence to her right and a grove of trees up on the next hill. She felt like she was on a boat, and the horse's head was the bow. Jasmine panted as she ran, and Serenity noticed that her own breathing followed the same rhythm.

A smile broke out across her face and she closed her eyes for a moment. No pressures, no gossip, no prying eyes. Just her and her horse and the Lord of all creation.

Thank You, she prayed. *For everything, even the people in my life that can be a bother sometimes.* Especially *for the people in my life.*

Having people care too much about you is better than having people not care about you at all. Serenity felt calm in her heart with this thought. She knew that she couldn't have everything all neat and tidy the way she liked it all the time when it came to people, but she could be glad that she had people at all.

She gripped the reins and pulled back a bit, slowing Jasmine to a trot. The horse blustered and shook her head. She still had some ride left in her, but Serenity knew she needed a rest.

The sun was tracking downward through the sky. There were still a couple of hours left before the sun went down, and when she wasn't moving so fast, she could feel the lingering heat in the Texas air.

"Let's head over to those trees," she said. Jasmine whinnied her approval.

Serenity guided Jasmine over to the grove of five white oaks. The trees were clustered together like friends sharing a whispered conversation. Their full-leafed crowns were dense and blocked out most sunlight around their roots, and some of the leaves were beginning to change colors.

When she reached the shade border, Serenity dismounted and slipped the bridle off of Jasmine's nose. The horse shook her mane and lowered her head to munch on the tall grass. Serenity patted her flank and walked slowly under the broad canopy, looking up at the thick mass of leaves and the jagged slivers of blue sky peeking through. The branches twisted as if they had been knitted together, creating a latticework that she could practically run through. In fact, she knew she could, because she had done so with Josh many times when they were little.

A quiet sigh escaped her lips as she sat down beneath the largest tree, nestling herself between two big roots. It was like being in a room with a vaulted ceiling and low windows. The leafy canopy soared over her head and the lowest branches began about eight feet above the ground, providing an unobstructed view of the grassy hills in every direction. Jasmine raised her head and brayed. Serenity smiled and waved at her, and the horse continued grazing.

Just like a little girl with her mommy...

Serenity touched the rough bark of the massive tree, letting the flood of memories wash over her. She hadn't been up this way for a while since it was on the southeast corner of the property, which was sort of diamond–shaped, so this was actually the farthest point from the house without going onto the neighbors' land. Mama didn't like it when she and Josh would come out here because it was out of sight from the kitchen window, but what kid could resist such a wonderful natural playground?

She and Josh would spend hours every summer scampering through the branches like monkeys and hurling acorns at one another in early fall. It was also in this very grove, actually beneath the slender tree to the left a bit, that Serenity shot and killed the deer that hung over the door at Daddy's store. But it was echoes of laughter, not gunshots, that she heard now as she listened to the wind rustle through the branches.

A tear trickled down her cheek and fell onto her jeans. She sniffled and squeezed her eyes shut. She hated when this happened – the tsunami of grief crashing into her, breaking her heart and ripping open the scars that hadn't yet healed, and probably never would. Of course, what did she expect by coming to this spot?

Still, even with the pain, it felt good to remember. She liked being where he had been, where he had walked, where he had played. He was gone but echoes of his joy, his laughter, the happiness she had shared with him still lingered like the faintest smoke.

She sat there in the shade for a while, listening to the memories, watching Jasmine graze, feeling the breeze slither through the leaves. When the sun started to dip low on the horizon, she picked herself up and walked over to the horse.

"Ready to head home, girl?"

Jasmine lifted her nose in what could be interpreted as a nod. Serenity hugged her neck. Josh was never big on horses, but he would ride with Serenity on occasion. Hillbilly was the only one who was around before he died.

"I wish you could have known him," Serenity whispered. Jasmine blew out through her lips and dipped her head.

"All right, little missy, don't be impatient." Serenity slipped on the bridle and fastened the buckle. She hoisted herself up onto the saddle and patted Jasmine's shoulder. "Let's head on home before Crack Shot and Hillbilly get jealous."

As she crossed the driveway on the way to the barn, Greg drove up in his Ford Expedition.

"Hey, sweetheart," he said, leaning out the window.

"Hey, Daddy."

"Had a good ride?"

Serenity nodded, squinting in the setting sun.

"Oh, I picked up your boots," Greg said, gesturing toward the box on the passenger seat. "Good as new."

"Thanks. Forty bucks, same as last time?"

"Nah, forget it. My treat."

Serenity smiled, telling herself not to worry. "Thank you, Daddy."

Greg smiled back, though there was concern in his eyes. "You all right, sweetheart?"

"I'm fine," she answered quickly, trying her best to hold his gaze. Why was he looking at her like that?

After a moment, Greg nodded. "Well, all right. I'll see you up at the house." He shifted into drive and paused. "Oh, I saw Miss Nancy at Marlow's. She was all abuzz about this ribbon you bought. You trying to catch someone's eye at the dance on Saturday?"

Serenity groaned and turned Jasmine toward the barn.

****

Thursday and Friday flew by. Serenity was busy with her kids in the mornings and early afternoons, and when she had some time to herself, she would read or mess around on her phone. She had an Instagram account and she would sometimes post pictures of herself with her horses, but she wasn't a compulsive selfie-taker like most people her age. She rarely liked how they turned out, and posting photo after photo of herself seemed vain. Besides, she didn't have many followers. She liked looking at other people's pictures more than her own. She followed several big names in equestrian sports, along with trainers, veterinarians, and teachers. Something would stir inside of her when she looked at these people and their big adventures. A voice deep within her heart told her that she should be a part of that world.

And another voice would usually pipe up. *What's so great out there anyway?*

When the internal back–and–forth would get too loud, Serenity would find something else to distract her, something not related to horses in any way. Much to her mother's delight, she had recently taken up cake decorating, and she was pleased to discover that she actually had a knack for it. Greg was also happy to have another culinary hobbyist in the house.

Serenity had never been big on traditional decorations like frills and lace and flowers. She was feminine, just not "dainty." She'd never had any reason to feel bad about it, nor should she, but when it came to cakes, she let her inner child romp and frolic, covering the cakes in swirls and dollops and flourishing calligraphy. Her creation Friday evening drew a gasp of surprise from her mother.

"We should bring this to church for the potluck," Patti declared. Serenity agreed.

Saturday morning was rainy and a bit cold. Streaks trickled down the windows as Serenity looked out at the roof of the barn. There wasn't any thunder or lightning so the horses would have no reason to be scared. But still, she didn't like that she was warm and dry in the house and they were out there in the barn, probably wondering if she was going to come out and see them.

After a few hours, she couldn't stand it anymore. She pulled on her rain boots, grabbed an umbrella, and headed out into the downpour. Despite her daddy's sprawling golf umbrella, she was half-soaked by the time she made it to the barn.

Brays and whinnies greeted her when she opened the door and stepped inside. She glanced up at the roof, noting a few small leaks. None of the water dripped into the stalls, though. She spent a few minutes with each horse, comforting them and feeding them horse cookies. She mucked the stalls, gave the horses some hay and oats, added water to their buckets and then stood in the barn doorway, watching the rain come down and form little rivulets on the ground that ran downhill.

Even though it was late October, the rain smelled like summer. The pitter-patter on the tin roof was soothing. Serenity took a seat on an overturned plastic bucket and watched the world get washed clean. She wondered if the Harvest Dance would still happen tonight. Probably would, since it was indoors and all, but she found herself thinking that she wouldn't mind if it got rained out. Then she wouldn't have any reason to wear that stupid ribbon. Why did she get it, anyway? Little girls wear ribbons.

It *was* a very pretty ribbon, though...

She looked over at Crack Shot. The brown dappled horse held her gaze for a few seconds before peeling back his lips and showing her his teeth. Serenity laughed.

"You're right. Ain't no reason to get all prettied up for no one in particular and then get all soaking wet. Looks like a night for hot cocoa and Netflix."

Jasmine brayed her agreement. Serenity gave her a nod of appreciation.

Hillbilly stamped his hoof, like he was trying to catch her attention. She frowned. "What's up?"

Hillbilly jerked his head toward the door. Serenity turned and her mouth fell open.

Right before her eyes, the rain vanished, as if someone had closed a tap. About thirty seconds later, spears of sunlight broke through the clouds and illuminated spots on the grass, much like Crack Shot's dappled hide. Serenity looked back at Hillbilly, but the horse didn't make eye contact.

"Really?" Serenity said to the fracturing clouds. "Is it that important that I go?"

The clouds parted and a shaft of direct sunlight stabbed into her eyes. She winced and turned away, giving the horses dirty looks as they whinnied their amusement.

"Y'all better hope I have a good time or I'll feed you mushy carrots from the back of Mama's crisper drawer in the fridge."

The horses fell silent and ate their hay.

****

Twilight came. Serenity stood in front of the mirror, scrutinizing her reflection. Patti stood behind her, her eyes sparkling with admiration.

Serenity tugged on her red–and–white flannel shirt.

"It's a bit tight in the chest area," she said with a frown.

Patti clicked her tongue. "You can blame my genetics for that."

Serenity gave her a smirk in the mirror.

"Of course," Patti added with a leering grin, "your father never complained none."

Serenity spun around. "Mama!"

Patti's expression was a mixture of amusement and arrogance. "The Lord's blessings fall upon whom He wishes. Wouldn't have minded being a few inches taller, though. I'm glad your father picked up the slack on that regard. You don't have to stand on your tippy–toes to get something out of the kitchen cabinets."

"Whatever you say, Mama." Serenity ran her hands down the sides of her legs, feeling the smoothness of the jeans hugging her hips. "You don't think the jeans are too tight? Might as well be painted on."

"Ain't no shame in showing how the Lord's blessed you, but you're a long way from showing all your cards. Trust me, sweetie, you'll probably be one of the more modest girls at the dance. Now turn around and let me look at you."

Serenity obeyed, not sure why she felt foolish. Honestly, she loved her outfit: a flannel shirt tied in a knot at her waist without revealing any skin, her favorite belt with her lucky buckle, and form-fitting blue jeans that eased into her freshly-soled Ariats. Her mama had helped her tie the ribbon at the back of her hair, letting the fabric trickle down with her wavy curls. She thought about wearing her black felt hat but that would hide the ribbon. It was strange how the ribbon was the part of her ensemble that she was most proud of, considering how much embarrassment it had caused her.

Patti was practically glowing. "You look like a dream," she said proudly before shouting, "Greg! Come in here and take a look at how lovely your daughter is."

Serenity rolled her eyes and then quickly threw on a smile when her father appeared in the doorway. A big grin split his face.

"Well good golly Miss Molly, you look beautiful, sweetheart."

"Thank you, Daddy."

"You want me to drive you?"

"Daddy, I ain't fifteen. I don't need an escort."

Greg raised his hands. "Just checking. It's a father's instinct when he hears the word 'dance.'"

"I know." She gave both of them a hug.

"Your friends going to meet you down there?" Patti asked.

"Yeah, but I don't know how much time they'll spend with me. Cassie said she's bringing along a 'friend,' and Kelly said she was invited to be someone's date just yesterday."

"Don't feel bad, sweetheart," Patti said, rubbing her arm.

"I don't, Mama. If anything, it'll give me an excuse to get out of there sooner."

"Now what kind of attitude is that to take to a dance?" Greg said.

Serenity sighed. "Sorry. I'm just still not sure about this. Seems silly."

"Until you get swept off your feet," Patti said with a wink.

"Or sit in the corner and play on my phone the whole time."

Patti stuck a finger in her face. "Now I'm going to see those girls at church tomorrow and I'm going to ask them if you behaved yourself tonight. I don't want to hear anything about phones or corners or any of that nonsense. I want you to have fun. Don't think of it as a fishing expedition."

"I don't. That's what you guys are doing."

Patti and Greg smiled at each other.

"We just love you, is all," her father said.

Serenity exhaled slowly. "I love you too. Y'all are the best."

Greg gave her a peck on the forehead and checked his watch. "Better get a move on. Fashionably late is one thing but late late is another."

Serenity tightened her stomach, wishing the butterflies would quit their fluttering.

"All right. I won't be out too late but I don't want to come home and see you two sitting by the doorway waiting for me."

"Who, us?" Patti said with feigned incredulity. "We are modern parents of a daughter who is fully grown, and we would never intrude – "

"Oh yes, you would."

Her parents smiled at each other again. "Yes, we would," Patti chuckled.

Serenity gave them both kisses on the cheek and grabbed her jacket off the hook before heading outside. When she turned around, she saw them watching her from the kitchen window. She waved them away, but they just waved back.

Dear Lord, she pleaded as she got in her truck, *please make it quick.*

CHAPTER FIVE

THE PARKING LOT was already pretty full when Serenity pulled up to the Jonesburg Roller Rink. Aside from the churches, it was the largest building in town for a gathering, and every year for the last twelve years, the rink was the location for the Annual Harvest Dance, sponsored by the Citizen Alliance of Jonesburg. The "Citizen Alliance" part was mostly hogwash, since the dance was financed by several of the more prominent businesses in the area. Greg had a banner put up a few years back. He didn't see any noticeable increase in business so he didn't bother to throw his hat in the sponsorship ring again, even though Patti told him that advertising is like a seed: it needs watering, time, and patience. Greg grumbled that his customers most likely wouldn't care a lick either way if his store's name was hanging on the wall while people square-danced and he wasn't going to throw away any more hard-earned money. Patti never brought it up again.

After she found a parking spot, Serenity sat in the truck for a moment, staring at the bright building. Underneath the roller rink sign was a large yellow banner with the words "12th Annual Harvest Dance." Two of those spastic balloon men that car dealerships like to use shimmied and waved as the fans at their base blew currents of air up through their slender bodies. Even though it was October, the entire facade of the building was wrapped in Christmas lights. That made Serenity laugh.

She remembered coming to the dance with Rick a couple of times, and once with Cal. The place still looked the same, the loud music coming from inside was pretty much the same, the people heading through the front door were the same. The only thing that felt different was her. And not just a little bit. It was like those memories belonged to someone else, someone who had gone away a long time ago. Her fingers twisted around the steering wheel.

What in the world am I doing here?

She started to shift the truck into drive when she heard a knock on the window. Cassie and Kelly's smiling faces peered through the glass.

Serenity pushed a smile through and opened the door. "Hey, darlings."

The girls gave her hugs. "We're so glad you made it," Kelly said. Serenity could tell she was just a bubbling bottle of energy waiting to pop, and a moment later, she knew why.

"This is Chris Dodson," Kelly said, grabbing the arm of the tall man beside her.

Serenity blinked. She had known Chris since middle school. And she also knew that he had gotten Amy Tremonti, the captain of the cheerleadering squad, pregnant and married her right after graduation. That marriage ended very publicly three months ago. And now here was Kelly hanging on him like a Christmas ornament.

"Pleasure," Serenity said, sticking out her hand. Chris took it with a smile. "How are the kids?" she added.

Chris cleared his throat and glanced at Kelly. "They're, uh, just fine. Adapting to life in Houston."

Serenity gave a curt nod and turned to Cassie, who also had her hand threaded through a man's arm. Her ex–boyfriend's arm. Barry Sikes, proud holder of the title of Most Outrageous Prankster in Jonesburg High School history. He and Cassie broke up last year after two years together. Looks like they had mended fences.

"Nice to see you again, Barry," Serenity said.

"You too, Serenity. Still playing with them horses?"

Serenity gave him a cold look. "Yep. Still *playing.*"

Cassie squeaked out an awkward laugh. "Let's get inside and get us some punch."

Chris motioned for Serenity to lead the way. She obliged, wishing once again that her jeans weren't so tight. At first she had been hesitant about going in. Now she couldn't wait to get inside so she could get away from these cuckoo birds.

Barry's hand shot out in front of her and pulled open the door for her. He smiled, showing off his tobacco-stained teeth. Serenity nodded her thanks and went in.

The first word that came to her mind was *noisy*. There was a bluegrass band up on a makeshift stage at the far end of the roller rink. The sprawling wooden floor was dotted by a dozen couples dancing in various styles, and some were pretty good. A man was spinning and sliding a woman around like she was a yo-yo attached to his hand. Beth Haversat was shaking her ample hips much to the delight of a young man who was way too close to her. In just a few seconds, Serenity could ascertain who was there with their companion in life and who was there looking for a companion. Most of the men wore hats and cowboy boots, and most of the women were dressed like she was, though there were plenty of less modest variations to be seen.

Mama was right. Serenity didn't feel so self-conscious anymore.

Someone tugged on her arm. Kelly and Cassie pulled her toward the punch table.

"Don't dance without us," Kelly said to Barry and Chris, who already looked distracted.

The three girls made their way over to the refreshment table and grabbed some plastic cups.

"You don't approve," Cassie said as she filled her cup with

punch and grabbed a few pretzels. "I can see it in your eyes."

"Come on," Serenity said, wishing she had at least a little more time to formulate her thoughts. "Y'all ain't little kids. Y'all can make your own decisions about who you spend your time with."

"Wish my mama was as laid back as you," Kelly grumbled.

"Well, your mama is a pretty sharp tack."

"See?" Cassie said to Kelly. "She doesn't approve."

Serenity didn't like the feeling that they were ganging up on her. "Guys, look, I'm not going to judge you for who you came here with. I just want all of us to have a good time."

Cassie grinned. Serenity had always been secretly jealous of her dazzling smile, and she could see why Barry found his way back into her orbit. Both Cassie and Kelly were beautiful and sweet. Serenity just hoped they weren't wasting their beauty and sweetness on a couple of losers.

Listen to yourself. You sound just like Mama when she's talking about you.

Serenity frowned at herself and downed a glass of punch. "Who wants to dance?"

A few moments later, the three of them were stomping and shimmying on the dance floor while the band played a rowdy bluegrass number that had the whole house rocking. Serenity caught a glimpse of Barry and Chris standing off to the side, their eyes riveted to the three of them in the center of the floor. Serenity didn't like the looks in their eyes. Maybe she should make it her mission to keep Cassie and Kelly away from them as much as possible tonight...

Someone tapped her on her shoulder and she turned around.

"Henry!"

A brown-haired young man with a stooped neck and a curled right hand smiled up at her.

"Hi, M–M–Miss Serenity."

Serenity glanced back at Cassie and Kelly. "Hi, Henry. Are you having a good time?"

"Yes, ma'am."

"You don't have to 'ma'am' me, Henry. I think you're a year older than me, anyway."

"Yes, ma'am."

She chuckled. "Do you like the music?"

Henry nodded. "Mm–hmm. Miss S–Serenity?"

"Yes?"

"Could you...I mean, could I have a d–d–dance with you?"

She hesitated for a moment, not wanting to leave Cassie and Kelly. But she saw the eagerness in Henry's eyes.

"Sure, let's dance."

She offered her arm and let Henry lead her to an open part of the floor. The song shifted to a more laid-back do-si-do style and Serenity took Henry's hand and gently spun around and pushed and pulled. Henry wasn't able to react quickly and she didn't want him to feel slow or uncoordinated, at least more than he already did. She saw the concentration in his face as he struggled to keep pace with her, holding onto her with his good hand and trying to match her steps. Despite the effort it took to do a simple dance, his face was bright and cheerful. Serenity gave him a warm smile and he looked like he had just won the lottery. She really hoped she wasn't leading him on but she got the feeling that Henry didn't have any serious feelings for her. He was just happy to be in her company.

She caught Cassie and Kelly's eyes across the room, and she could see that they were touched by her kind gesture. Then Barry and Chris snuck up behind them and they forgot all about her. Serenity pursed her lips as she watched the boys dance too close and put their hands where they shouldn't. Why was it so easy for good Christian girls to forget their decency and modesty at the snap of a finger?

Well, you're one to talk. Don't pretend like you haven't crossed boundaries.

A shadow of shame passed over her heart. She had crossed her boundaries, and she still wore the scars from the pain that had followed...

"Miss Serenity? Are you okay?"

Serenity looked at Henry and gave him a weak smile. "Yeah, I'm just a little tired. I ain't danced in a while and I forgot what hard work it is."

"Do you want to rest? D–do you want me to get you some water?"

"No thanks, Henry. I'll just go and sit a spell. I spotted your old teacher, Mrs. Herschel, over by the bandstand. Why don't you go and see if she'll let you sweep her off her feet?"

Henry beamed. "Thank you for the dance, Miss Serenity!"

"My pleasure, Henry."

Henry shuffled off and disappeared into the swirl of bodies. Serenity made her way toward the rows of chairs lined up against the wall and sat down. She looked around at the smiling faces and swinging hips and blinking lights and the spinning disco ball hanging from the ceiling. She knew most of the people she saw but they weren't exactly "friends." Cassie and Kelly were out of sight, and she wondered how long they would be friends after this. It wasn't hard to see where their lives might be headed, and it would certainly be a different road than the one she was on.

Serenity crossed her legs and folded her hands on her lap. It's strange how you can feel completely alone in a room filled with people. She didn't particularly dislike anyone, the music was nice, and the atmosphere was vibrant and energetic. But she couldn't quite put her finger on it; she just knew she didn't belong here.

A young man wearing a denim shirt and a trucker hat approached her and asked for a dance. Serenity politely refused, and the young man tipped his hat and walked off. Thirty seconds later, she saw him dancing with Beth Haversat.

Her thoughts started drifting to her horses. Were they warm enough? It wasn't a cold night but she still worried about them. Perhaps she should skedaddle and check on them. Yes, that's what she was going to do.

She stood up and searched the floor, looking for Cassie and Kelly again but still not finding them. She did spot Henry dancing with Mrs. Herschel. He grinned and gave her a thumbs-up. Serenity returned the gesture, glad he was having a good time. She tugged on the knot on the front of her shirt and sighed. Mama would probably chastise her for coming home so early, but she wasn't going to sit around wasting time just to keep up appearances.

She took one step toward the door when she heard a voice behind her.

"Serenity."

Every muscle in her body locked into place. The air in her lungs turned to ice. Her heartbeat thundered in her ears.

She had heard wrong. The music was too loud and had messed up her hearing. There was no way that voice belonged to...

She blinked, turned around, and blinked again.

"Rick."

The young man standing in front of her was a couple of years older than she was. Two years, five months, and seventeen days, she knew precisely. When she had last seen him four years ago, he was a cocky eighteen–year–old with a dashing smile and a shock of light brown hair. Now he was lean, toned, with a strong chin and a hard mouth. A three–inch scar trailed down his right cheekbone. His mesmerizing green eyes, though, were still the same – soft, mysterious, playful. They were the first things she had noticed about him when she first met him back in eighth grade, and they still captivated her attention now.

Her tongue felt like it was made of rubber as she tried to form words. "Wh–what are you doing here?"

Rick grinned shyly and looked at his boots. "Well, it's a bit of a long story." He narrowed his eyes at her, and Serenity suddenly had the awful feeling that there was something wrong with her appearance. Was her makeup smudged?

A warm smile crossed Rick's face. "You look good."

Serenity frowned in confusion. "Thanks. So...what are you doing here?"

Rick looked at his boots again. "I don't know what your plans are right now, but do you want to catch up? Maybe get some coffee? I saw that Naughty Latte is still open."

Serenity blinked once more. Her mouth hung open, trying to form words that refused to coalesce. Finally she found her voice.

"No. No, Rick, I don't want to get coffee and catch up. And I do have plans, in fact. I'm going to get out of this stupid place and go home and go to bed, and I don't want to see you or hear from you.

Okay?"

Now it was Rick's turn to look dumbfounded.

"Serenity, wait!"

He reached out to her as she stormed off, pushing through a group near the door and stumbling out into the cool night air. The temperature change took her breath away and she gasped, feeling queasy. Gulping a deep breath, she took off running through the parking lot, nearly slamming into her truck. Her hands trembled as she searched through her keys to find the right one. After unlocking the door, she yanked it open and dove into the cab, slamming the door behind her.

Her fists clenched the steering wheel until her knuckles were white. Thoughts and feelings and worries and hopes and fears collided in her brain, creating such a ruckus, it was giving her a headache.

Rick was back.

Here.

Now.

In that gaudy building in front of her.

The doors to the roller rink flew open and Rick appeared. His handsome face was creased with worry. Serenity's eyes widened and she threw the truck into reverse. The tires spun and kicked up gravel as she floored the gas pedal.

Rick heard the commotion and looked straight at her.

"Serenity!"

Clenching her teeth as tight as she could, she shifted into drive and sped off into the night. She thought she heard him call her name again but she wasn't sure.

Why was he here?

WHY WAS HE HERE?

Serenity could feel her whole body vibrate with each thundering heartbeat. Her eyes were fixed on the dark road stretching into blackness but his image was burned into her mind.

He had always been a good-looking guy but seeing him just now, he was *gorgeous.* Now that she had put some distance between them, she let her mind's eye wander and explore. His muscles filled out his black t-shirt and his legs looked strong and sturdy in his faded jeans. She hadn't gotten a good look at his hands but she could still remember how gently his fingers had brushed through her hair and stroked her chin when he would lean in to –

The blaring semi-truck horn startled her out of her reverie and she yanked the steering wheel to the right, shrieking with terror. She pulled her truck into her lane just in the nick of time. The semi bellowed its anger as it rumbled past.

Serenity pushed her hair out of her eyes and panted for breath. She needed to get home. This night had been a huge mistake.

Please please please, she prayed, *let this all just be a bad dream...*

****

Patti looked up from her mystery novel and glanced over at Greg. He was fast asleep in his favorite chair, head thrown back, mouth hanging open, hunting catalog spread out across his expansive stomach. He snorted and made a funny gurgling sound and closed his mouth for a moment only to let it fall open again. Patti laughed silently as she started to turn the page. She sat up straight when lights whisked across the living room and a car door slammed shut.

The front door flew open, startling Greg out of his sleep. Patti craned her neck just in time to see Serenity march past the living room and up the stairs. Patti gave a confused look to her husband, who still seemed disoriented, then got up from her chair.

"Serenity?" she called out.

The answer was a slamming door. Patti flinched, turning around and staring at Greg, who looked just as baffled as she did.

****

Serenity looked at the clock beside her bed. 11:47 pm. The darkness of her room surrounded her like a cocoon. The blinds were drawn shut and the curtains closed. The darkness felt warm, safe. She had been trying to fall asleep for hours but her mind was such a jumble, sleep was impossible. But at least the darkness gave her the quiet she needed to sort out her thoughts.

She had been afraid that her mother would come to her room and ask her if she wanted to talk. She knew it had certainly crossed her mother's mind – how could it not? – but thankfully no one knocked on her door. The morning would be a different story, of course, but for now, she just wanted to be alone.

The red colon on the clock between the minutes and the hours seemed to blink more slowly than usual. She watched the clock for what felt like at least a couple of minutes, and finally the time switched to 11:48. She groaned and burrowed her head into the pillow. It made her mad to be buffeted by her feelings like this. Serenity Hope MacAlister wasn't an emotional, reactionary, fainting–couch teenage drama queen. She was strong, even–keeled, self–reliant, an entrepreneur...

Her fingers gripped the pillow and she sighed into the fabric.

...and a girl whose heart had been broken numerous times, and just when the scars were starting to heal, this guy shows up and rips the skin wide open again.

Serenity felt her cheeks flush with heat. He had some nerve! He must have known that showing up like that would upset her. Probably did it on purpose. No call or text, nor had he dropped by the house. No, he just materializes out of thin air at a dance that she didn't even want to go to. How did he know she was going to be there anyway? He knew her well enough to know that she wouldn't go to something like that unless someone twisted her arm. In this case, Mama. Did *she* know Rick was in town? Were they in cahoots? Did Daddy know, too? Did they string along Cassie and Kelly to make sure that she would be there? Was *everyone* in on it?

She extracted her face from the pillow and looked at the clock. 11:51. She rolled over and stared at the ceiling. Another groan rumbled in her throat, sounding more like a growl.

Why?

Why did he have to be back? Why couldn't he just stay gone? And most importantly, why did she still care so much? It was more than four years ago when she had last laid eyes on him. Four years is a long time... Long enough to fall in and out of love again, long enough to start her own business, long enough to watch her dreams fizzle and fade.

But not long enough to forget about Josh. And not long enough to forgive Rick.

No amount of time would ever be long enough for that.

CHAPTER SIX

THE RIDE TO CHURCH the next morning was a quiet one. Greg drove Patti's Mazda sedan, with Patti sitting in the passenger seat and Serenity in the back. In fact, the whole morning had been quiet. Serenity had said hardly more than a "Morning" when she came down for breakfast. Patti looked like she was wound tighter than a spring but she held her tongue. Greg sipped his coffee as nonchalantly as he could, which meant he wasn't nonchalant at all. Serenity just kept her head down, thanked Mama for the sausage and biscuits, and ate in silence.

She felt bad keeping her folks in the dark like this, but she just didn't feel like talking about last night. The crazy conspiracy theories bouncing around in her head had dissipated by morning, and seeing the worried expressions on their faces convinced her that her parents had no idea about Rick. She was going to have to tell them eventually, though. Seeing Rick would be just as jarring for them as it was for her, though not entirely for the same reasons. Should she warn them now, in case they saw him around town? She didn't want her mother to come home in tears or her father to sulk in sullen anger because they suddenly saw the fellow who was with Josh when he died.

Whenever the right time was, it wasn't now. Serenity stared out the window, watching the hills and fields dotted with trees and houses. It was a beautiful day, a few degrees warmer than yesterday. A perfect day for a ride. She felt a little guilty thinking it, but she couldn't wait for church to be over so she could get out on the grass. Then she remembered that this Sunday was the church's monthly potluck and her heart sank. Ordinarily, she would be thrilled, because there were some mighty fine chefs in the congregation aside from Mama. Jim Laramie probably had his big ol' smoker out in the field right now, and its aromas would compete with the pastor for the congregation's attention. Nan Pacer's sweet potato casserole would surely make an appearance, as would Gretchen Van Der Jorn's Brunswick stew. And of course, she had forgotten about her own cake. She hoped Mama had put it in the trunk before they left.

Despite her mood, thinking about all the delicious food she could eat after the service made her mouth water. Maybe she would be feeling a little better by then. She leaned her head against the window.

Doubt it...

Greg turned off the road up the gravel driveway that led to

Saving Grace Baptist Church. The church building looked like something out of a Norman Rockwell painting: tall white steeple, white wooden siding, two heavy double doors. It was the third oldest church in town and the only one to survive the twisters in '78, so technically it was the oldest standing church building. Serenity had come to this church practically every Sunday since she was born, and she knew that her parents had been attending years before she arrived. It was like a second home to her. Most people would probably wrinkle their nose in contempt at the simple structure and lack of contemporary church elements like a youth group or professional worship band or pre–K program. There were other churches in town with bigger buildings, bigger budgets, bigger congregations, and they were all good places filled with good people. But there was something about Saving Grace Baptist Church that felt right to her, and not just because it was more traditional or old–fashioned than other churches.

It felt right because the Word of God was preached from the pulpit every Sunday. Pastor Avery Johnson wasn't a showman or an orator, but he had the gift of teaching, and he knew he could never say it better than God could, so he let God's Word do the talking. Many people preferred Sunday sermons that were more like motivational speeches or spiritual pep rallies for the week ahead with a few verses sprinkled in here and there. Serenity had visited churches like that, and though she knew there was nothing wrong with that kind of service, it felt like empty calories to her. Every Sunday at Saving Grace, she came away from the service with something new to ponder about God and His holiness.

After Greg found a parking spot, she got out of the car and shielded her eyes from the morning sun. Off in the distance, she could see the smoke rising from Jim Laramie's barrel smoker. The air was heavy with mouth-watering aromas, and virtually every pair of hands was holding a dish wrapped in tin foil, heading toward the kitchen to let their food stay warm during the service.

Patti touched her arm. "Brought your cake, sweetie. It's in the trunk."

"Thanks, Mama," Serenity said, giving her a brief smile. "I'll take it inside."

"I'll do it, sweetie. Why don't you and Daddy go grab our seats. I need to find Art Calhoun and make our trade."

She opened the trunk to take out the cake, rye bread, and corn fritters, her own contribution to the potluck. Serenity took her father's arm and the two of them walked toward the church in silence, though just before they reached the steps, he looked at her with a comforting smile and patted her hand. Serenity knew what he was saying as if he had said it out loud.

"I'm here for you, sweetheart, whenever you're ready."

Serenity smiled back.

"Thank you."

Pastor Avery was waiting at the door, shaking the hand of everyone who came inside. He shook Greg's hand and nodded to Serenity.

"Welcome, MacAlisters. Is Patti with you? Don't tell me she's still at home, cooking."

Greg jerked his thumb over his shoulder. "She's bringing the cake in. Serenity made it, in fact."

Pastor Avery's eyes lit up. "Well, amen to that. You have the finest teacher in Texas, young lady."

"She reminds me all the time," Serenity said with a grin.

Greg gave her a smirk. "Be nice, now."

"Come on, Daddy, you know it's true."

"I do, but you won't hear me admit it more than once."

Pastor Avery patted them both on the shoulder, gently ushering them inside. "We'll all look forward to enjoying your culinary delight, Miss Serenity."

"Thank you, Pastor Avery."

She followed her father into the sanctuary and they found their usual seats, over by the wall on the left side, just a couple rows in front of the middle. An usher handed them bulletins, and Greg set his down on the chair next to him to save the seat for Patti. Serenity browsed the paper without reading it. She spotted Cassie a few rows up, sitting with her folks and younger sister. Barry was nowhere to be seen. Serenity couldn't see Cassie's face but she could tell by the way she hung her head and let her shoulders droop that she wasn't in the best of moods. Looks like last night hadn't turned out to be such a fairy tale for either of them.

She glanced around the sanctuary. Kelly wasn't here. That girl never missed church unless she was seriously ill. Serenity frowned. She didn't want to jump to conclusions but –

"Thanks, sweetie." Patti eased into the seat next to her and gave her shoulder a squeeze. She leaned in close. "You know you're going to have to tell me what's going on sooner or later."

Serenity closed her eyes and inhaled slowly. "I know, Mama. I just need a minute."

"Sure, sweetie. Take all the time you need."

"Wait, didn't you just say – "

"Good morning, church!" Pastor Avery proclaimed from the pulpit with a cheerful smile.

"Good morning!" the congregation echoed back to him.

Serenity tried to concentrate on the opening prayer and the announcements and the worship songs, but she just didn't feel like her heart was in it this morning. When the last song was sung, the congregation sat down. As Serenity took her seat, she looked to her left for no particular reason. Her eyes became as wide as dinner plates.

Rick Stevens was sitting three rows back. He was looking right at her, giving her a cautious smile. Serenity froze again, her rear hovering a few inches off of her seat. She felt Mama touch her back and ease her down.

"You okay, sweetie?" Patti asked. She apparently didn't see Rick.

Serenity's throat felt like sandpaper. "Yes," she breathed, looking straight ahead. "I'm fine."

The sermon was about something in the book of James, but Serenity hardly heard a word. She spent the next thirty–five minutes fighting the urge to look to her left, but she was terrified that if she did, she would see Rick looking right at her. Or maybe he would be looking at the pastor and ignoring her completely. She didn't know which was worse, but she couldn't risk finding out. Either possibility would be too embarrassing. It was torture, though. First he shows up at the dance, and now he's at church.

At church! Before the army and Josh and everything, she didn't know if Rick had ever set foot in a church. Which was one of the reasons why her parents were so against their relationship back then, and now that she had had plenty of time to reflect, they were absolutely right. What on earth was she thinking, going out with a troublemaking high school senior who didn't seem to care about God or the Bible or his own salvation? She should have known better than that. But he was so handsome and charming and exciting and...

"Please bow with me in prayer," Pastor Avery announced.

Serenity bowed her head, though she didn't close her eyes. As the pastor prayed, she turned her head slower than molasses. She couldn't stand it anymore – she had to take a look.

Rick's head was bowed and his eyes shut. Serenity watched him for a few moments, strangely hoping that he would open his eyes and look at her. His eyes remained closed, and she closed hers as well. After the prayer, the church worship team, consisting of a guitar player, a drummer, and Art Calhoun on the fiddle, led the congregation in one more song, and then the pastor dismissed everyone with a joyful exhortation and a reminder to head out to the field adjacent to the church for the Annual Autumn Potluck Bonanza. Pastor Avery seemed to take particular delight in pronouncing the word "bonanza."

Serenity rose to her feet. She looked over her mother's shoulder to make eye contact with Rick, hoping her expression was stern enough.

Patti noticed the strange look on her face and started to turn around.

"Mama," Serenity blurted, bringing Patti's attention back to her. "Can you help me take out the cake outside? I saw one of my kids and I need to mention something to them."

"Of course," Patti said with a smile.

Relieved, Serenity turned to her father. "Jim Laramie's smoker looks pretty impressive, doesn't it? Is that the same kind you were thinking of getting?"

Greg knitted his eyebrows. "Hmm. I didn't get a good look at it. I'll go check it out."

"Great. See you out there."

With her parents safely diverted, she turned toward Rick again. He was greeting some folks in the congregation, though he gave her a quick glance that said, *what are you waiting for?*

Serenity made her way over to him, pausing for a moment to say hi to Heather. She didn't want to lie to Mama, after all. Squeezing past Mr. and Mrs. Cranston and greeting Old Mr. Harold, she stood toe–to–toe with Rick.

He looked at her with those deep green eyes and gave her a smile that made her knees weak.

"Good morning, Serenity."

This might have been church, but to heck with politeness. "Rick," Serenity declared, "what are you doing here?"

"You mean at Saving Grace?"

"Yes, at Saving Grace! At the Harvest Dance. In this town. Why are you here, Rick?"

Rick looked at his feet. "I'm sorry, Serenity. I know this is a bit of a surprise. There's a lot I need to tell you..."

"Are you here because of me?"

"What?"

"Just tell me the truth. Are you trying to get back together?"

Rick opened his mouth to speak, then stopped and looked over Serenity's shoulder. Serenity turned around.

Pastor Avery gave them a smile and offered his hand to Rick.

"Mr. Stevens."

Rick shook the pastor's hand. "Pastor Avery."

"We're happy to have you with us this morning."

"Thank you, sir. I really enjoyed your message. I've been reading through the book of James in my morning devotions and your message shed some light on things I've been pondering."

"Oh, well I'm glad to hear that." Pastor Avery looked at Serenity. "Miss Serenity. See y'all outside?"

Serenity and Rick nodded. Pastor Avery nodded as well, the smile still plastered on his face. After he was gone, Serenity turned back to Rick and placed her hands on her hips.

"Since when do you read the Bible?" she demanded.

"I said there's a lot I need to tell you."

"Rick, my parents are here. Never mind how I feel; think about how *they* would feel."

"I know, Serenity. That's one of the reasons why I'm here. There are things I need to say to them too."

"So you just decide to show up at church today? You just came to crash the potluck?"

"Of course not. You know there's no easy time for any of this."

Serenity fumed but she knew he was right. There was no good

time for Rick to suddenly reappear in her life.

"Look," he continued, "I don't want to upset you. This is weird for me too. But there are things I need to tell you, and your parents too. Everyone, in fact."

Serenity glared at him, trying to rein in the conflicting emotions stirring in her heart. "Fine," she said, tossing her hair and hoping she looked sufficiently annoyed.

"Thanks," Rick said with a grin that melted her icy indifference in a heartbeat. "I'm not going to stay for lunch. I don't want to upset anyone, at least not more than I already have. But I talked to Pastor Avery and he wants me to speak to everyone before we eat."

Right on cue, Serenity's stomach rumbled. If that wasn't embarrassing enough, she felt her cheeks become warm. Judging from Rick's amused expression, they were probably glowing bright pink. Resisting the urge to cringe and hide her face, she stood up straight and looked him in the eye.

"Okay. But I want you to know that I'm really not okay with this. Last night at the dance and showing up here too... No one likes to be blindsided."

"I'm sorry, Serenity, I really am. Things are different now and I need people to know that."

Serenity narrowed her eyes. "Different how?"

Rick gave her an infuriating wink. "Let's go outside."

Serenity shook her head and then turned around to head out of the church building. As she walked ahead of him, she felt a bit self-conscious, wondering if he noticed that she was ten pounds heavier than when they had been together. She quickened her steps to get outside as fast as she could without looking like she was rushing. Then she slowed down so she would seem relaxed and nonchalant about the whole thing.

Get a grip, Serenity!

She clenched her teeth and walked with what she hoped was a normal gait, glad when she made it outside. The field to the right of the church was already full of people, and the smells of delicious Texas cuisine filled the autumn air. A gentle breeze whispered across the fresh-cut grass, probably the last time it would be trimmed that year. The sun was bright and the sky was a deep azure blue. It was a lovely day, except for her ex-boyfriend standing behind her. She turned around and gave him a stern look.

"I'm going to go over to my parents and tell them you are here. You can go find Pastor Avery and say your piece. And depending on what you say, I'll decide if I want to talk to you some more."

Rick nodded. "Fair enough."

Serenity watched him walk around the edge of the field. She chewed on her bottom lip and let out a long, slow breath. He was making it really hard for her to stay mad at him, even though she had every right to be. And he was right – there *was* something different about him. Something in his eyes. A softness that had never been there before. He had always been a bit of a firecracker, always hungry for life, never satisfied, full of zest and enthusiasm. But now he seemed to be more at peace.

Maybe because he's found serenity.

She smothered a groan. She had definitely inherited her father's penchant for lame puns.

Patti and Greg had already gotten their food. Several tables were lined up to make long tables and Patti and Greg were sitting on the end. Greg saw his daughter coming and stood up.

"Serenity, you want me to get a plate for you?"

"No, thanks." Serenity sat down and looked at her hands. "Mama, Daddy, I need to tell you something. You'll know in a minute anyway." She took a breath. "Rick Stevens is back in town."

Patti blinked. "What?"

"He's back in town. He's here now, in fact. I saw him inside just a few minutes ago. He said he's going to say something to everyone."

At that moment, there was a pop and a squeak from the speakers set up under a tent off to the left. Everyone turned to see Pastor Avery standing with a young man with his head bowed. Serenity looked at her parents. Patti's hand was on her chest. Greg's face was like a statue.

"Folks," Pastor Avery said, holding the microphone up to his mouth and fidgeting with the cord. "We're going to bless this food in a minute, but before we do, there's someone I'd like to introduce to you." He put his hand on Rick's shoulder. "This here is Rick Stevens. Many of you know him, many of you don't. He grew up in our fair town and has spent the last four years fighting for our country in Afghanistan. He's just returned home and he called me the other day and wanted my advice on...well, on how to say what he's going to say. I told him that this would be the best time to do it, since we're all gathered together. Rick..."

He gave Rick the microphone. Serenity held her breath as she watched him take it and look up at everyone staring back at him. There was an awful moment of silence. Then he cleared his throat.

"Howdy, y'all," he said, his voice strong yet somehow fragile. Something in Serenity's heart stirred when she saw him so vulnerable like this. Her surprise, her hurt, her anger, all was pushed aside for the moment. More than anything in the world, she wanted to know what he had to say.

Rick glanced at Pastor Avery and cleared his throat again. "I'm, uh, I'm Rick Stevens. Like Pastor Avery said, I grew up here. I just finished my tour with the Marines in Afghanistan...Oorah...and it's good to be home. Many of y'all know who I am, though probably not for the right reasons. I raised a lot of hell when I was young. Well, younger. And I know I hurt a lot of people. One incident in particular. I don't mean to dredge up old mud or reopen old wounds, but I want to make amends any way I can. I'll leave y'all to your fine food but I just want to say that by the grace of God, I'm not the person I was before. If I've hurt you, I hope that I can come to you and ask your forgiveness. I don't reckon I'll be in town for too long, but I would be humbled if you would let me sit down with y'all sometime and you can lay your pain on me. Lord knows I deserve it. Well, that's all I got to say for now. Thanks for listening, and enjoy the rest of your day."

He handed the mic back to Pastor Avery and walked off toward the gravel parking lot. Serenity followed his every step until he disappeared from view. He didn't turn to look at her. Everyone stayed quiet until he drove off, and then a low murmur arose from the tables.

Serenity looked at her mother. A tear rolled down Patti's cheek. "Mama," she whispered. "You okay?"

Patti sniffled and nodded vigorously. "Yeah, I'm okay."

Greg reached out and touched her hand. Serenity saw the pain in his eyes as well. She looked out at the dirt driveway that led out to the road. Wisps of dust still lingered in the air. She didn't hear Pastor Avery ask everyone to bow their heads so he could bless the food. She just stared at the dust, watching it blow across the grass.

CHAPTER SEVEN

THE FRONT DOOR CREAKED as Greg pushed it open. He waited for Patti and Serenity to shuffle inside and then he closed it behind him. The women looked at him. Greg stroked his chin and stared vacantly into the corner.

"Let's have a seat in the living room," he said quietly.

Serenity sat down on the love seat. Patti sat next to her and Greg settled into his favorite chair. A strange, sad silence hung over the room. Patti reached across and took Serenity's hand.

"Sweetheart, did you see Rick at the Harvest Dance last night?"

Serenity nodded.

"Did he say anything to upset you?" Greg asked, leaning forward.

"No," Serenity answered. "I was getting ready to leave and then all of a sudden, there he was. Like a ghost standing right behind me."

"What did he say?"

"He said that he was back in town and that he wanted to catch up. He asked me to go to the Naughty Latte with him for a cup of coffee. I told him 'no.' I...actually told him more than no."

"What do you mean?" Patti asked.

"I told him that I never wanted to see him or hear from him again."

"Looks like he took that to heart," Greg said wryly.

"I saw him sitting in church this morning," Serenity went on. "I was afraid that y'all might see him but thank God you didn't."

Greg leaned back in his chair and folded his hands across his belly. "So how do you feel about all this?"

"I don't know," Serenity said with a shrug. "How do *y'all* feel?"

Patti and Greg looked at each other. "To tell you the truth," Patti said, "a small part of me is glad that he's back, though I don't know what he meant by 'just being in town for a little while.' I know the accident wasn't his fault, at least not directly, but I think we all blame him to one degree or another. And we weren't the only ones who lost someone. The Conways and the Aggers lost their boys too. But I never really realized until now that I've been carrying around a grudge against him all this time and I've lived long enough to know that grudges are poison. I don't know what I'd say, but I'd like to talk with him." She turned to Greg. "What do you think?"

Greg held up his hands and blew out a long breath. "I don't rightly know myself. Crazy how quickly the mud gets stirred up by one small catfish. But you're right, dear. I've been holding onto my anger against that boy this whole time. He ain't no innocent victim but he doesn't deserve our anger. It ain't fair and it ain't Christian. And he showed a lot of courage getting up in front of folks like that today. He seems sincere about wanting to clear the air and hear us out, and I think we should give him the chance."

Silence descended again like a curtain. After a long, uncomfortable minute, Greg leaned forward. "What about you, darling? I think your take on all this carries the most weight."

Serenity stared through the living room window, watching the red and orange leaves twist in the breeze.

"I talked to him after the service," she said, her voice barely more than a whisper. "He said that he wouldn't bother me again if I didn't want it. And at first, I was going to take him up on that. But hearing y'all's thoughts makes me think that he does deserve at least a chance to clear the air like you said, Daddy. I've been carrying around my own anger like y'all have, but I've also been carrying my own guilt. I know y'all never liked him, and now that I'm a little older and a little wiser, I know that he wasn't right for me. But I can't shake the feeling that if I had known that back then, maybe...maybe he and Josh never would've..."

She couldn't hold back the sobs. Tears spilled through her fingers as she buried her face in her hands. Patti leaned across the love seat and embraced her daughter's shivering shoulders. Greg rose from his seat and cradled both of them in his big, strong arms. Serenity gripped her mother's blouse and wept against her chest as Patti hushed her and stroked her hair.

All of the guilt and shame came pouring out of her. If she had never gone against her parents' wishes and gone out with Rick, they would have never ended up alone in his truck back behind the old movie theater that warm summer night. They would have never started making out, and Rick never would have pressured her to go a bit further. Serenity never would have had to adamantly refuse, and Rick never would have angrily driven her home. Josh would have never met them on the front porch, and he and Rick never would have left to go to a party on the other side of town. Serenity never would have watched her brother and her boyfriend speed off into the night. The police never would have showed up at their house several hours later, blue and red lights casting long shadows through the windows. Mama would have never screamed and collapsed into Daddy's arms when the officer told her that Josh had been driving drunk with three friends and had run off the road, resulting in his own death and the deaths of two of the boys with him. Serenity never would have stumbled numbly into the kitchen, feeling like a ton of bricks was pressing on her chest. She would have never felt her heart break and her whole world shatter in an instant.

But it happened. By some miracle, Rick had survived only with a nasty gash on his face, but Josh and two other boys were gone forever and there was nothing she could do about it except weep for him, weep for her parents, weep for herself. Weep for her selfishness and stupidity. It was her fault that Josh was dead. Deep down, no matter what people might say, she knew it was true. And right now, she hated herself for it.

"I'm sorry," she wailed, hot tears pouring down her cheeks. "I'm so sorry..."

"Sweetheart," Patti whispered, tears spilling from her eyes as well, "it's not your fault. It's not your fault, sweetie."

Greg sniffled, his eyes shimmering. "Your mama's right, darling. None of this is your fault. Don't blame yourself."

Serenity nestled against her mother's chest, feeling her warmth. Her strength. And Daddy's gentleness. The tears began to subside as soothing waves of comfort washed over her. She wanted to stay right there forever, surrounded by love.

The three of them remained in their embrace for a few minutes, then Patti pulled back and looked at her.

"We love you, Serenity Hope."

"I love you too, Mama and Daddy."

Greg handed her a box of tissues from the end table. Serenity grabbed several and blew her nose loudly.

"Sorry," she mumbled into the tissue. "I know I've got an ugly cry face."

Greg smirked. "Not going to lie. You kind of do."

Serenity snorted, and that helped release the weight smothering the room. She wiped her nose and eyes and slowly regained her composure, as did her mother. Greg looked at the two of them with a warm smile.

"Well," Patti declared as she dabbed at her eyes, "that was eventful."

Serenity nodded and sniffled once more.

Patti gave Greg's hand a squeeze. "I think some sweet tea is in order."

"Amen," her husband said.

She headed off to the kitchen and Serenity looked sheepishly at her father.

"I didn't mean to fall apart like that," she confessed.

"Don't feel bad, darling. I wish you had told us sooner. That's an awful weight to be carrying around like that all these years."

"But it's true, though, right? At least in some small way? If it weren't for me, Rick and Josh wouldn't have become buddies and they wouldn't have gone out that night."

"You don't know that, sweetheart. Our lives are in God's hands. It's a cliché but it's true. We can't go through life thinking, 'If I had done this...' or 'If I hadn't done that...' And anyway, that kind of thinking doesn't change the fact that Josh ain't with us no more."

He put his hand on her knee and looked right into her eyes. "I've done plenty of frettin' and fumin' at myself, at God, even at your mama. But I never once blamed you for anything. I want you to know that."

Serenity felt the tears coming back. "Thank you, Daddy."

She hastily wiped her eyes as Patti returned with a tray of glasses filled with sweet tea and ice. They all took quiet sips. Patti set her glass down and folded her hands in her lap.

"Well, seems as though Rick is helping to clear the air and he ain't even here."

Serenity frowned. "I don't know if that's a good thing, Mama."

"Of course it is, sweetheart. And I'm more sure than ever that we should sit down and have a chat with him. If we've been carrying around these burdens, so has he. But I'll leave it up to you, Serenity. I don't want to push you into something you ain't ready for."

After a moment of hesitation, Serenity nodded. "I'll talk to him. I think it'll be good for both of us."

"You sure?"

"Yeah, I'm sure. I'm still mad at him for showing up out of the blue like this but that ain't no reason to give him the cold shoulder like I did. I just wasn't really enjoying myself last night and that was the nail in the coffin."

"You didn't have a good time?"

"No Mama, I didn't have a good time going to a dance alone and watching Cassie and Kelly get felt up by their exes and everyone else act like mule deer in heat."

Patti's eyes grew wide. She looked at her husband with incredulity. "Well, Lord have mercy. What's happening to this town?"

Greg shrugged. "Same thing that's happening everywhere. They need to bring back chastity belts, in my opinion," he added as he eased himself up out of his chair. "I'm going to go fix the sink upstairs. All this cryin' is making me question my manhood."

"Ain't nobody questioning that, honey," Patti said. She gave her daughter a smile. "Feel better, sweetheart?"

"I do. Thanks, Mama. It's been an emotional weekend."

"I'll bet."

Serenity gazed out of the living room window. She could just barely see the barn roof past the grassy hilltop.

"I think I'll take Crack Shot out for a ride."

Patti straightened her blouse. "I think I'll go with you."

Serenity's eyebrows rose. "Really?"

"Sure." Patti leered at her. "Why, don't think I can handle a horse in my old age?"

"Of course not, Mama. I just remember you saying...never mind. But take Jasmine. Hillbilly's always been a bit skittish around you."

"He ain't still sore about the time I tripped and poked him with the carrot stick in his—"

"Yes Mama, he's still a bit sore about it."

Patti huffed. "Well, he can hold his grudge all he likes. He can also pout in his stall while we have fun with the other horses."

Serenity grinned. "Let's go."

****

"Woohoo!"

Patti was all smiles as she gripped the reins with one hand and held onto her hat with the other.

"Hang on, Mama!" Serenity called over her shoulder. She leaned forward, urging Crack Shot to kick it into high gear. Despite his young age and occasional feistiness, Crack Shot seemed to have an instinctive connection with his rider, no matter who the rider was, and would respond almost intuitively.

"Slow down, sweetie!" Patti called after her.

"No, you speed up!"

Patti squared her jaw and snapped the reins. "Get 'em, girl!"

Jasmine stretched out her neck and broke into a gallop. Patti yelped again as she chased after Serenity and Crack Shot.

Serenity's hair flew around her face as she pulled the horse into a hard right turn and sped off along the top of the hill. She could hear Jasmine's hoofbeats pounding the grass behind her. No way she was going to let Mama win.

The two women and their horses chased each other over the

low hills and down into the shallow valleys. It took them just a few minutes to cross their fifty–acre property and reach the far fence that bordered the Fairbaughs' land. Serenity pulled back on the reins and Crack Shot reeled to a halt just before he collided with the fence. A moment later, Patti and Jasmine rode up, though Jasmine's stop was a bit more graceful.

As they both panted for breath, Serenity looked at her mother. The two of them wore big, silly grins. Patti took off her hat, which had miraculously stayed on top of her permed hair, and wiped her sweaty brow.

"Golly, I need to do that more often."

"You used to," Serenity said.

Patti gripped the saddle horn and looked off into the deep blue horizon. "Yes I did... I guess having Aunt Lillian around made it more comfortable for me when we were younger. You know I don't like to do things alone."

"So why don't you come ride with me?"

A red hue crept over Patti's face. "I guess you're just so amazing with these animals, I feel foolish whenever I'm out with you. Like an old man trying to beat his grown son at basketball."

"It ain't a competition, Mama. It's just for fun. And you rode Jasmine pretty well for not getting in the saddle for a couple of years. If you want to do something, Mama, just do it. Don't think about how you look or what others think." Serenity frowned at the strange expression on her mother's face. "What?"

Patti shook her head. "Nothing. Just amazed at what an incredible young woman you've turned out to be."

"I was bawling like a baby inside just a little while ago."

"That has nothing to do with you being an incredible young woman. In fact, it makes you even more of one."

Serenity smiled. They stood side–by–side on their horses for a few minutes, surveying the rolling hills. Land that hadn't been touched by a plow or combine. Land that had been in the family for three generations...

"Mama."

"Yes, sweetheart?"

"Are we in trouble?"

Patti's head snapped to the side. "What makes you say that?"

"I saw some letters on Daddy's desk a while back, Mama. I know I shouldn't have looked but I did. Daddy says he's optimistic about the tourist season but the store isn't bringing in enough to keep up with the mortgage, is it? Plus the county is looking to hike the tax rates again."

Patti squinted in the sun and opened her mouth to answer. But she stopped, mulling her words carefully. Her shoulders sagged and she let out a quiet sigh.

"You're not a child anymore so I ain't going to lie to you. Things aren't looking good right now. We were trying to find the right time to tell you but there never seems to be one. And it don't mean that we're about to get tossed out on our rears, so don't you go worrying yourself over something that might not even happen. But you're right, the money isn't enough. I'm probably going to have to go back to work."

"Mama, no! You know you can't stand up for too long."

"I'll find me a sitting job."

"No, Mama. You need to stay home and take it easy. What good will it do if you get sick again?"

"What choice do I have?"

Serenity sat up straight. "I can sell some of the horses. I only need one for my classes. And I can start paying rent. It ain't fair for me to live off y'all like a kid."

"I won't have none of that," Patti insisted, raising her chin. "These horses are your family just as much as your father and I, and you don't sell off family to pay the bills. And I won't take none of your money for rent, either. We already talked about this, sweetheart. You need to save your money for horsemasters school. Aunt Lillian keeps asking me when you're going to go up to Nebraska and work for her. You could bring the horses, work, and go to school. Make a life for yourself. Honestly, sweetheart, this land is too much for your father and me. It's big, it's beautiful, it has our family history in the soil, but it's just land. What are we going to do with fifty acres that we don't use? It makes for a pretty picture, but not when the taxes are double what they used to be fifteen years ago."

Serenity couldn't believe what she was hearing. "You can't sell this place, Mama! Where would you go?"

"We ain't going nowhere, sweetheart. Your daddy's been talking to Isaac Fairbaugh and he'd like to buy the land to expand his grazing pastures. He'd let us live on the land and pay rent, and we wouldn't have to deal with the mortgage and taxes and all that."

"Rent the home that you already own? Become tenants in your own house?"

"Nothing's final, sweetie. But we have to be realistic. And if we don't have the land for riding around on fine days like this, it makes sense to go on up to Aunt Lillian's, because there won't be any sort of life for the horses here with all them cows around."

Serenity's vision swam with tears. Her lip trembled as she clenched the reins in her white-knuckled fists. "Sounds like you and Daddy have my life all planned out."

"Serenity..."

Before her mother could say another word, Serenity snapped the reins and galloped down the hill. Her tears made the breeze sting her eyes and she wiped her sleeve across her face. She was too angry to think. She was too angry to pray. She was almost too angry to breathe. All she could do was ride.

Her mother found her at the barn, sitting outside of Hillbilly's stall. Patti didn't say a word as she led Jasmine into her stall and poured some grain into her bucket. Beets was perched on a ledge and she stroked the purring cat for a moment. Taking cautious steps, she walked over to Serenity and sat down beside her. They sat in silence for a couple of minutes.

Patti wiped the tears from her daughter's cheek. "Say what's on your heart, sweetie."

Serenity stared into space, her jaw clenched. Her nostrils flared and she said, "This is our *home,* Mama. This is where I grew up. Where Josh grew up. Where these horses have spent most of their lives. I don't want to leave it. I don't want to leave you and Daddy."

"I know you don't," Patti said, pulling her close. "And I don't want you to think that we're pushing you away. We just want what's best for you. Your father and I don't want to hold you back from living your own life. I've seen it happen too often, to my friends growing up and to their kids as well. I always told myself, 'My children aren't going to be the kind that get stuck where they are and never get out to follow their dreams.' You're capable of so much, Serenity. You are going to do amazing things."

"Thanks, Mama, but it's my choice to decide what those amazing things are. Maybe it's here, maybe it's not. Maybe going out to live with Aunt Lillian would be a good choice, maybe not. But I have to make that choice on my own. I have to be the one to decide what my dreams are. I'm happy here, Mama. I really am. There ain't nothing wrong with a quiet life in a quiet town."

"You're right, sweetheart. You're absolutely right. Forgive me; I'm a mother, and mothers think too much about their children's futures. Your father and I love you more than anything. Don't ever forget that."

Serenity squeezed her tight. "Don't worry, Mama. I never will."

Patti wiped away a stray tear and smiled. Then she pointed a finger in Serenity's face. "And none of this 'paying rent' talk, young lady. You keep saving your money to take care of these animals and for your future. Now if we're still having this conversation in ten years, then we might have to make some kind of arrangement."

Serenity laughed and slapped the dust off her jeans. "Oh, Mama..."

Patti drew her lips in a thin line. "Speaking of which, what are we going to do about Rick Stevens?"

"I don't know," Serenity said with a sigh. "I don't even have his number. I'm guessing Pastor Avery's got it, so I'll ask him. I still can't believe that he just got up in front of everybody like that today."

"What do you think he meant by him not being in town for long?"

Serenity shrugged. "Can't say for sure. I don't think he's got any family around. His folks and his sisters moved away somewhere after he joined the Marines. I'm guessing he's staying with a friend."

Patti nodded slowly. "Probably. It feels strange to say it, but he turned out to be quite a handsome fellow, didn't he?"

"Mama..."

Patti held up her hands. "I'm just saying that the army really cleaned him up and filled him out. When you and he were an item, he always wore those baggy clothes and his hair was always a mess. Honestly, I don't know what you ever saw in that boy."

Serenity's eyes fell to the floor. "Me neither."

Patti leaned down so she could look at her face. "Does it hurt to see him again? I'm not talking about Josh and the accident. I mean...does it stir up old feelings?"

"Mama, that was ages ago. I was just a junior in high school. Besides, after that whole mess with Cal, those kinds of feelings are going to be dead and buried for a long time."

"Oh sweetheart," Patti said, pulling Serenity close again. "It breaks my heart to see your heart broken. It'll get better sweetie. Trust me, it will."

Serenity wiped her eyes. "I hope so."

CHAPTER EIGHT

"LOOK AT ME, Miss Serenity!"

"Good, James! Keep a tight hold of those reins."

Serenity shielded her eyes from the sun as she watched the nine–year–old boy ride Jasmine around the arena for the first time without help. His wide eyes and bright smile warmed her heart, something Serenity sorely needed after yesterday's bombshells.

"You scared?" she asked.

James shook his head. "It's like she knows what I want her to do, like we're telepathically connected or something."

Serenity laughed. "Well, there's some fancy words. It's called a 'bridle' and 'reins,' buckaroo, not telepathy. But you're right – she does know what you're thinking. She can tell if you're scared or relaxed, if you want to take it easy or ride hard and fast."

"I don't want to ride hard and fast," James said, looking a bit nervous. "Nice and easy is good right now."

"And Jasmine knows it. Just keep a tight grip, don't let her head dip too far but don't pull back either or she'll stop. Know what, let's give that a try. Ease back on them reins a bit."

James obeyed, pulling Jasmine to a halt. He grinned again. "I don't want to drive a car. I want a horse!"

Serenity walked up and patted Jasmine's flank. "If it were up to me, every car in the world would be stacked up high in a big ol' pile and we'd all be riding horses."

"Like in the cowboy days?"

"Yep."

"With guns and outlaws and things?"

Serenity raised an eyebrow. "Well, what can I say? This is Texas."

Tires crunched on the gravel driveway leading up to the barn. Serenity squinted, then beckoned to the boy.

"Folks are here. You want to show them your progress?"

"Sure!"

The large black pickup trunk stopped under the oak tree and a man and woman got out. Every time she saw them, Serenity was struck by how picture-perfect James' parents always looked. His dad was tall, handsome, with salt-and-pepper hair peeking out of his Stetson, always well-dressed in a classic Western style. His blonde wife was just as beautiful, fashionable yet still casual. They looked like the kind of folks that took expensive vacations but also enjoyed backyard barbecues. Not to mention that their son was the typical all–American boy. Whenever she looked at them, Serenity felt something stir inside her. Not jealousy, just cautious hope. Hope that one day she might have the handsome husband and bright–eyed children and look like she had just stepped out of a Western fashion magazine. It seemed silly and more than a little vain, but she couldn't help it. And it was certainly possible. These people in front of her were proof.

"Howdy, Miss Serenity," James' dad said as he walked up.

Serenity tipped her hat. "Morning. How are you, Mrs. Trent?"

The woman gave her a quick smile and looked over Serenity's shoulder. "James, honey, come on down. We need to get going."

"Oh, he wants to show you what we learned today," Serenity said. "He's really proud of himself."

"That's nice. James! Let's go."

Serenity glanced at Mr. Trent, who looked off to the side. She wasn't sure what was going on but she knew better than to pry. She went over to to the horse and helped James down.

"I wanted to show them the trot," he whined.

"Next time, sweetie," Serenity said quietly, noticing his parents standing coldly apart. "Why don't you go give your mama a hug?"

The boy sulked and dragged his feet through the dusty arena. His dad opened the gate and the boy shuffled over to his mother, giving her a half–hearted hug. Mrs. Trent put her arm around his shoulder and led him to the truck without a word.

Serenity eased up to the fence where Mr. Trent was standing. He looked sort of lost.

"Same time next week?" she asked.

Mr. Trent toed a rock with his boot. "Um, I don't think so, Miss Serenity. We're going to have to stop James' lessons."

Serenity blinked in surprise. "Oh sir, please don't do that. He's improved so much over the last month, and he loves the horses. You should have seen him today when he rode Jasmine for the first time without my – "

"I'm sorry," Mr. Trent interrupted. "We're just going to have to stop."

"Is everything okay?"

Mr. Trent looked back at the truck. His wife and son were already inside. James waved at him.

"Not really," Mr. Trent answered. Serenity could hear the frustration and uncertainty in his voice. "But we'll manage. We don't want to take James out of your program. I know he enjoys it and it's been good for him, helping him with his behavioral issues at school and at home. We just..."

His voice trailed off, and Serenity had a terrible feeling that he was going to cry. She flinched when he stuck out his hand. "Thank you for everything you've done," he said curtly. He turned on his heel and marched back to the truck. Serenity watched them drive away, then walked over to Jasmine. She swung the reins down over her head and led her out of the arena over to the barn.

She felt like a deflated balloon. That was the second family to cancel classes in the last month. As Serenity eased the horse into the stall and unbuckled the saddle cinch, she thought about what her mother had said yesterday about going up to live and work with Aunt Lillian. If two more kids pulled out of her classes, she wouldn't be making enough money to take care of the horses here, and she sure wasn't going to put that burden on her parents.

She looked up at the clouds, noticing the wispy patterns and shapes.

Lord, is this what You want me to do? You know how much I love this place, but if You're taking me somewhere else, please let me know without any big surprises. You know I don't like left turns in my life like that. Please show me what You want me to do, and give me the strength to do it.

Jasmine stamped her hoof to say, *"Finish taking off my saddle!"*

Serenity grinned and obeyed. "Sorry, girl. Just lost in my thoughts."

Hillbilly and Crack Shot whinnied. Serenity got the distinct impression that they were laughing at her.

"You think it's funny now," she scolded them, "but just you wait and see how it is up at Aunt Lillian's. Your life of ease and luxury will be over, misters. Mm–hmm."

The horses dipped their heads and munched on some food.

Serenity smirked victoriously. She went to the barn door and looked down over the pasture, following the winding driveway that connected to the road like a creek that feeds into a river. Across the road were more hills and fields, the Fletchers' place, with a row of pines acting as a windbreak off to the left. And beyond that was blue sky and cotton clouds stretching all the way to heaven.

Serenity inhaled a deep breath, picking apart the smells that drifted into her nostrils. Grass, leather, manure, dirt, wheat, and sunshine. She loved those smells. When she closed her eyes, she could "see" them in her mind. That didn't mean that she couldn't find those smells elsewhere, but not the same mixture.

Just thinking about leaving made her heart break. It was one thing to be a sixteen-year-old girl with one horse and big dreams and a supportive family, but it was another to be twenty years old with a dead brother and a twice-broken heart and three horses and aging parents and a home slipping through their fingers.

She leaned her hand against the door frame and lowered her head.

Lord, please show me what to do...

The phone in her pocket buzzed. Her heartbeat quickened as she pulled it out, and she immediately told herself to calm down and be reasonable. The sunlight glared off the screen and she held it close.

It was a message from Pastor Avery.

Howdy Miss Serenity. I wanted to apologize if yesterday was uncomfortable for you. Many folks have questions and I'm sure you do too, but I'm telling everyone to talk to Rick about it. I don't want to be in the middle. If you want to reach out, his number is 940-555-3497. God bless.

Serenity stared up at the sky.

Really? Now?

A cool breeze caressed her face and stirred her hair. She exhaled loudly and looked at her phone again. Her thumb hovered over the screen for a few moments and her stomach twisted itself in knots. She glanced over her shoulder. Hillbilly was looking right at her. He waved his nose and shook his head.

Serenity shook her head, too. James was right – these animals *do* know what we're thinking. Squaring her jaw, Serenity dialed the number and held the phone to her ear. It rang once, twice. She tapped her boot on the ground, hoping Rick wouldn't pick up. But then she would have to leave a message. What should she say? He wouldn't have the number in his phone so she could just hang up. But what if he called her back? Should she leave a message or not?

Rick's voice came out of the speaker next to her ear. "Hello?"

Serenity's mouth hung open, her lips moving aimlessly. She swallowed what felt like a rock in her throat, then winced. He probably heard the disgusting sound over the phone.

"Rick," she stated in her most professional voice. "It's Serenity."

"Hey, Serenity. I'm glad you called. I wasn't sure if you were going to or not."

"Well, I did."

"I can see that." His laugh was like cool stream water. "So what's up?"

"You tell me. You said that you have lots of things to say, and I guess I'd like to hear them."

"Good. When are you free?"

"What's wrong with right now?"

"Listen Serenity, I don't want to sound weird or make you uncomfortable, but I'd really rather talk to you face-to-face. This ain't the kind of stuff you just say over the phone."

Serenity was quiet for a moment. She ground the toe of her boot into the dirt. Better get this over with sooner rather than later.

"I'm free right now."

"You are? Great. You want me to come over or you want to go somewhere in town?"

"Where are you now?"

"I'm at my uncle's place on 441."

"Why are you there? He ain't lived there for years."

"That's one of the things I'd like to tell you."

Serenity licked her dry lips. Why was her heart beating so fast?

"I'll come out there," she said. "I don't know if my folks are ready to see you yet and I don't want people in town to see us together and start their yammerin'."

"Um, okay. I'll be here all day. Come over any time."

"I'll be there in one hour."

She ended the call and slumped against the door frame.

What was she doing? Going out to see him by herself? What if someone found out?

She clenched her fists and growled quietly.

Doggone it all.

"Wish me luck," she said to the horses as she closed the barn door. They whinnied their support.

When she entered the house, Patti was putting away some groceries in the fridge.

"Hey there, sweetheart. I was just about to fix up some sandwiches."

"No thanks, Mama," Serenity said on her way up the stairs. "I've got something to do in town."

She went to her room and shut the door. She took a quick shower to wash off the day's dust and changed into a fresh flannel shirt and jeans. After blow-drying and brushing her hair, she looked at herself in the mirror. Should she wear makeup? Nothing too flirty, maybe just some eye shadow and lipstick?

No. She wasn't getting all prettied up for her ex. He should be lucky she didn't come over there all dusty and sweaty. With a defiant nod, she marched toward the bedroom door and opened it. She paused when she spotted the sky blue ribbon laying on the desk. The ribbon she had been wearing that night at the dance. Maybe it wouldn't hurt if she –

She clenched the doorknob. Absolutely not. No makeup, no ribbons. In fact...

She went to the closet and grabbed her old Stetson. Rick had always told her how beautiful her hair was. Well today, she wasn't going to give him the opportunity. She put on the hat and left the room.

"You sure you don't want to stay for lunch?" Patti called from the kitchen when she came down the stairs.

"I'm sure," Serenity answered as she tugged on her boots.

Her mother came out of the kitchen holding a spatula. "Well, don't you look pretty."

"No, I don't, Mama."

"Of course you do. You always do. You going to be gone long?"

"I hope not." Serenity finished putting on her boots and opened the front door.

"Serenity."

She stopped and looked back at her mother.

Patti gave her an encouraging smile. "Be careful out there."

Serenity felt something prick at her heart. She knew her mother knew where she was going. Still, she had to keep up the facade.

"I will, Mama. Love you."

"Love you, too."

Serenity got in her truck and drove down the driveway. When she reached the road, she paused.

Was she really doing this?

Oh, stop being a baby.

She floored the accelerator, kicking up gravel behind her and fishtailing onto the road. Her mother's admonition to be careful popped into her head and she slowed down a bit. She was already a bit volatile; no need to be reckless with a two-ton vehicle.

The drive to town took exactly eight minutes, and it was another seven to get through the town's four traffic lights. When the storefronts and municipal buildings receded in the rearview mirror, grassy fields stretched out in front of her once more. She reached the turnoff onto 441 and headed east. It had been a while since she'd been on this side of town. There was nothing special between here and Arkansas. She used to come out this way when she was in high school because she used to go with Rick to parties down by the riverbank. Thankfully it never got too crazy, usually just a few beers and maybe a cigarette or two. Serenity never took part in that, and she always made sure Rick never had too much, either. She knew that sometimes he would get a little rowdy with his friends when she wasn't around, and she also knew that what they were doing wasn't right, but there was something exciting about being with someone who skirted the rules like he did. He wasn't *bad,* not like many of the other boys she went to school with, but he wasn't completely good either.

So what was he now? Serenity kept her eyes on the road ahead but her mind started wandering. He was clearly different. Appearances, for one thing – more muscular and well-groomed. Of course, four years in the military will do that to any man. And the way he talked and carried himself seemed more grown-up as well. She was more grown-up too, though not in all of the ways she wanted to be. The more she thought about it, the more distant those two people seemed to be. Four years is a long time, especially when you're only sixteen and eighteen years old.

But is it too long?

Serenity gasped and spun the wheel to the left, almost missing the dirt driveway hidden among the tall grass. The truck bounced as it hit a series of potholes. Serenity frowned, keeping a firm grip on the wheel. She had only been on the property once before but she remembered it being kept up. From the state of the driveway and the waist-high grass, it was clear that this place had been neglected for a while.

The spread was about the size of her family's land, though much more flat and better suited for farming. Everything was all overgrown, and it was impossible to tell what the crops once were. About a quarter of a mile in from the road stood a humble two-story farmhouse. As Serenity drove up, the house's poor condition became more apparent. Missing siding, broken windows, hideous bushes.

And right in the middle of everything was Rick Stevens. He was wearing a camo baseball cap and a white sleeveless t–shirt streaked with dirt. He was standing over what looked like a window shutter resting on two sawhorses.

He looked up when Serenity pulled into the yard and parked next to an oak stump.

"Howdy," he said as she got out, waving at her with a gloved hand.

Serenity waved back, immediately feeling foolish. She folded her hands together and walked toward him with slow, measured steps.

"What's all this?" she asked.

Rick wiped his brow and looked at her with a squint. "Well, the short version of the story is that this was my uncle's place, as you already know. He died while I was deployed. He didn't make a will so the executor let anyone take it who wanted it. I took it, paid a nice sum to everyone in the family, and now the deed is in my name. I'm going to fix it up and sell it for what I hope is a tidy profit."

Serenity chewed on her lip. "I'm sorry about your uncle."

Rick waved her words away. "He was a mean ol' cuss who didn't do nothing about it when the doctors told him he had liver cancer. In fact, I think he started drinking more. Maybe he just wanted to speed up the process."

"What about your folks?"

"My dad's down near El Paso and my mama and my sisters are up in Colorado where my grandma lives. Don't think they have much of a mind to come back here. They tried to talk me out of it."

Serenity cocked her hips. "Why didn't you listen to them?" She heard the accusatory tone in her voice but she didn't care.

Rick pulled off his work gloves and slapped them on his jeans. "Because I need to ask forgiveness."

Serenity stood still for a long time, her eyes riveted to his. Words formed and died on her tongue, and a long, deep silence stretched out between them.

"What happened to you?" she said finally. She knew how it sounded, and this time, she worried that she might have hurt his feelings.

"Let's sit on the porch," he said after a moment.

Serenity glanced warily at the house. "Is it safe?"

Rick shrugged. "Hasn't collapsed on me yet."

"How about just the front steps?"

"Fine by me."

Rick sat down on the third step up and Serenity sat on the step below his. After checking for protruding nails, of course. It felt kind of weird for him to be sitting behind her like this but she didn't want to sit on the same step with him, and he seemed to have the same thought. She turned her body and propped one boot on the step so she could look up at him.

"Well, I'm listening."

He opened his mouth, then sprang to his feet.

"Oh shoot, I'm so rude. Do you want a water?"

Before she could refuse, he bounded down the steps and opened a cooler next to the sawhorses. He grabbed two bottles of water and opened one for her.

"Thanks," she said, taking a small sip.

He unscrewed the cap of his water and took several gulps. "Don't mention it," he said as he wiped his mouth. "Now, where were we?"

"Um, you were about to spill your guts."

"Right." He replaced the bottle cap and stared out across the sea of grass. "I suppose I should say that my time in the military had more than one effect on me. I mean, you knew how I was. It definitely wasn't my idea to enlist, and my folks were so glad to see that I was going to get whipped into shape...I suppose it made me rebel even harder, knowing that my days of being my own person were numbered. And just like in the movies, Uncle Sam broke me down and put me back together. They had us running real dangerous missions over there in Afghanistan. Real bad sometimes..."

His words trailed off and he hung his head. Serenity leaned

forward to make eye contact.

"Hey," she said with a voice that was stern yet soft, "you ain't over there no more."

"I know," he said with a nod, looking at her with gratitude in his eyes. "Well, I suppose the best way to put it is that I found God."

Serenity kept her eyes on him, waiting for him to explain what he meant. He seemed to be choosing his words very carefully.

"I know it sounds so cliché, a soldier in a death zone, bullets and bombs everywhere. Kind of like a prisoner comes to Jesus because they got nothing else. And maybe in the beginning, it was just out of fear. But as I read my Bible and started meeting with the chaplain, it became real. I gave my life to Christ one year and three months into my tour of service, and it's changed me more than anything Uncle Sam ever did."

"I'm glad to hear that, Rick," Serenity said in an even tone.

Rick gave her a smirk. "I know you're skeptical, just like everyone else at base. I was a bit of a hellraiser in my early days, but I'm telling you, when God worked His saving grace through me, I truly felt like a new person. I was still Rick Stevens, and I still had a job to do, but I didn't have the same fear, the same need for acceptance, the same guilt that had defined who I was before. And what it also did was make me realize how much I needed to ask the forgiveness of those I've hurt. Starting with you."

Serenity rose to her feet. "Don't give me any BS, Rick. Why are you really here?"

"I came back here to see you."

"Just to see me? Just to ask my forgiveness?"

Rick opened his hands. "Well, sure. Serenity, I don't have any illusions about us getting back together. We're different people now. At least, I know I am. Four years is a long time. Heck, you probably have a boyfriend or a fiancé now anyway."

Serenity gave him a cold glare that she hoped made him uncomfortable. "What about you?"

"What about me?"

"Do you have a girlfriend or a fiancée?"

Rick blushed. Serenity instinctively tightened her stomach.

"No," he answered. "At least, not now. I suppose not ever, really, since we broke up."

Serenity exhaled slowly. She was strangely relieved. Why?

She sat down and took another sip of water. She was so bad at trying to play it cool. "Sounds like there's a story in there."

"Not much," Rick said with a pitiful laugh. "I, uh, started getting letters from Julie Warscham."

Serenity's eyebrows flew up. "Julie Warscham from high school? 'Just–Ask–Julie'?"

Rick blushed again. It made him look so doggone cute. Serenity took another sip of water.

"Yeah," he said. "'Just–Ask–Julie.' Though I should throw out a disclaimer: I never asked. I was faithful to you, I hope you know that."

"I do," Serenity said. Warmth spread through her chest.

Rick played with the water bottle cap. "Anyway, after I got deployed, she started writing me letters. I was kind of surprised because I didn't have much contact with her in school, but she said she'd always had a crush on me and had hoped that I would 'ask.' I suppose the fact that I didn't ask stoked her interest in me. So we became pen pals, I guess you could say. Then we started doing Skype and video chats. I'll spare you the details but let's just say that she made it clear that she considered me more than just a pen pal.

"And then when I became a Christian, I was convicted about our interactions and I told her that we needed to take things down a few notches. That didn't sit well with her. I didn't hear from her for a while, and then I got an email – not a handwritten letter like before – just an email saying that she was engaged to a fellow from Phoenix. That was the last I heard from her."

Serenity glanced up at the sky. "Hmm, I always wondered where she went. So why weren't you on social media or anything? It was like you dropped off the face of the earth."

Rick shrugged. "I thought about it but I kind of liked being gone, making a fresh start. I thought about you a lot; you and your folks and many other people in this town. I wondered what y'all were doing, what y'all thought of me, if y'all even thought of me at all. And I knew I could get those answers in a few mouse clicks. But something held me back. I suppose I was scared of what those answers might be. And when I made the decision to come back and get in touch with people again, I didn't want to do it through technology. I wanted people to see that I'm sincere face-to-face."

"So what do you want from *me*, Rick?" Serenity asked, rising to her feet again. "Do you want me to say that I forgive you? That I don't blame you for Josh's accident? That you broke my heart but it's cool because it made me into a stronger person? That I'm so happy that you're now my brother in Christ and invite you to Bible study? What, Rick? What do you want?"

Rick looked surprised at her outburst. He set the water bottle down and kneaded his hands.

"I don't know, Serenity... I don't want anything from you, I guess, unless you want to give it. But I do want to ask your forgiveness. For Josh's accident, for being a silly jerk who ran around doing stupid stuff and should probably be in jail now, for trying to push you too far that night, for killing what we once had together. I'm truly sorry, Serenity. I can't change anything or fix what I've done or bring your brother back. But I'm sorry and I beg your forgiveness. And if there's anything I can do to make it up to you in even a tiny way, I'll do it a hundred times over."

"Well, you can't." Serenity threw the water bottle to the ground and stomped over to her truck. Rick started walking toward her but she gave him a fierce glare that stopped him in his tracks. He watched with sad eyes as she put the truck in gear and drove away from the house. She looked at him in the rearview mirror, standing in the swirl of dust, watching her drive away.

It was only after she made it onto the main road that she let the tears flow. She pulled over on the side of the road and rested her head on the steering wheel. Tears trickled down her face and fell onto her jeans, making dark circles.

After a few moments, she looked at her face in the rearview mirror. She had the ugliest crying face of anyone she knew. She hastily wiped her eyes and stared out at the open road.

Stop it. You're stronger than this.

She took a deep breath, put the truck in drive, and pulled back out on the road. It was still early enough in the day that she didn't have to get home yet for her afternoon lessons.

There was someplace she needed to go.

CHAPTER NINE

THE TRUCK'S WHEELS CRUNCHED softly on the gravel as Serenity pulled into the cemetery. Large oak and willow trees shaded the scattered gravestones. Some stones were old and worn; some were new with names freshly etched. Serenity drove very slowly, as if she were afraid to disturb those at rest.

She couldn't see anyone else around, though there was a freshly–dug grave with a wreath and a cover off to the left. She wondered who it was. She didn't know everyone in town but she knew someone who knew someone who knew someone, so in a way, she *did* know everyone.

Josh's grave was a little ways up a small hill, so she parked at the bottom and got out. She stood still for a moment, taking in the smell of the autumn grass and the crisp fallen leaves. The sun was bright and a few birds chirped from the trees. Serenity never liked to come to the cemetery on days that were gray or rainy, but on a day like this, despite the sorrow, it was peaceful.

She glanced around at the older tombstones, wondering if anyone still came to visit them. Or if anyone even knew they were here. It didn't matter one way or another – the body was just an empty shell and the soul was elsewhere. Still, there was something profoundly sad about a person being gone and no one caring about it enough to stop by once in a while.

There were several tombstones with fresh flowers and that warmed her heart. It also made her wish she had brought some flowers. Mama would stop by once a month to bring flowers and clean Josh's stone. *"Even though he's not here anymore, he needs to look presentable,"* she said. Daddy would come with her sometimes, but Serenity knew he couldn't handle the grief like Mama could. Serenity was his baby girl, but Josh was his prince. The last male in his family line. He would come up here to Josh's grave sometimes, but it was usually on his own, and he usually didn't tell anyone.

Serenity always knew when he would visit, though. There would be something different about him when he would come home, something in the way he walked, the way he spoke, the way he ate. It would just last for the evening and the next day he would be back to his usual self. But on the days he had visited this grave, Serenity could see the yearning that was left empty in his heart. His prince would never grow up to be a king. That's what would cause the change in his demeanor – remembering what once was and would never have the chance to be anymore.

It broke her heart to see her parents try to cope with the sorrow. It was one thing for her to lose a brother, but they lost their son. Their firstborn, only son. They still had her, and they showered her with affection, but there would always be an empty place in their hearts. Hers, too. Josh was only a year and a half older than she was, and he was everything to her. He wasn't a perfect little angel, and perhaps that made Serenity admire him even more. After Rick entered the picture, he and Josh became good friends in the blink of an eye. At the time, that made Serenity feel a little bit better about dating Rick despite her parents' misgivings; she had introduced a new friend to her brother.

Guilt started rearing its ugly head in her soul again and she looked up at the cloudless sky.

You're here for Josh, she told herself, *not to throw another pity party.*

She took a deep breath of sweet autumn air and walked up the gentle slope to the cluster of tombstones. Joshua Benjamin MacAlister's headstone was off to the right, next to a few old stones that were so weathered, the names were hardly legible. She was glad that Josh was next to people from generations past. He had always been a history buff – he loved 19th–century American history. Davy Crockett, the Alamo, everything that made Texas proud. That boy loved his home state and he was a pure Texan through and through.

Serenity blinked away a tear and forced a smile as she sat down next to the stone.

"Hey there, goober," she said, looking at the wilted flowers. She wanted to toss them out but she knew Mama would want to be the one to do it. Josh never cared a lick about flowers or any of that "girly stuff" anyway. His room was always filled with rocks and arrowheads and animal bones that Mama was constantly throwing out when she discovered them on his shelves.

Serenity let a few moments pass, listening to the gentle rustle of the leaves and feeling the soft caress of the wind.

"Sorry I ain't been around for a while," she said, looking at the headstone. "I ain't going to make any excuses. But I think about you every day. You know that, right? I went to our tree spot the other day. Remember that time you fell from the branch and got your underwear stuck and gave yourself that monster wedgie? You should be glad that smartphones weren't around then because I would have snapped a dozen pictures and sent them to everyone I knew."

She toyed with a small twig in the grass. "There's, uh, something I need to tell you. I'm not sure how to deal with it. Him. Deal with him. He's not an 'it.' He's... Rick Stevens is back in town. Just showed up out of the blue. He blindsided me at the Harvest Dance, and then he shows up at church the next day. Yeah, Rick Stevens was in church. I about had a heart attack. And I'd be lying if I said that he didn't look mighty handsome. He was already heading into the army before the accident, but he and his family high-tailed it out of there pretty quick. And now, four years later, he just up and appears like a ghost. Thing is, though, he's changed a lot. He looks different, of course, but he ain't the same Rick. Not just more mature and all, but...he says he's a Christian now, and he came back to ask forgiveness. He says he wants to speak with everyone that he's hurt, but I get the feeling that I'm the biggest reason why he's back, since he hurt me in more ways than one.

"So I guess I'm asking, should I forgive him? I know it's the Christian thing to do, but I got to be honest: if he were here now and I said, 'I forgive you,' I wouldn't mean it. Deep down, I still blame him for the accident, even if your stupid behind was the one that was driving. I'm still mad at him for taking you away from me. And at the same time, I still have feelings for him. That whole mess with Cal really tore me up, though. I feel pulled in so many directions. I want to forgive him, I want to stay mad at him, I want to give him a second chance, I want to tell him to get lost."

She reached out and touched the smooth marble. "And no matter what Mama or Daddy or Pastor Avery or anyone says, I know it's my fault that you're gone. No matter what the Bible says, no matter how much I pray, I can't shake this guilt inside of me. Rick has asked me to forgive him, but how can I forgive him when I can't forgive myself?"

Her words trailed off and she rested her head between her knees. She didn't want Josh to see her cry.

A cool, comforting breeze stirred her hair and she looked up and wiped the tears away. She turned her attention to the trees while she composed herself, then she turned to the headstone again.

"Sorry about that. It's been a rough few days. I found out that we're in danger of losing our home. Daddy's business can't keep up, and I'm doing all I can to not be a burden, but Mama won't let me help out with the expenses. Though if my kids keep dropping out, I won't have hardly nothing to contribute anyway. And the way Mama tells it, she and Daddy are kind of throwing in the towel, thinking of selling the land to the neighbors and paying rent to live in our own home. Can you believe that? Mama said she thinks it would be a good idea for me to go up to Aunt Lillian's and take the horses. That was my plan anyway, but that was before the accident changed everything. It's been more than four years, I've got two more horses, and I don't know if I can leave this place. Too many memories, good and bad."

She brushed a strand of hair out of her eyes and chuckled to herself. "I'm a real chatterbox today. Sorry, brother. I just don't really have anyone to talk to about all this. Even my friends are acting all weird. I just wish you were here, Josh. You always had good advice. Though I wish you had told me to stay away from Rick. I would have listened.

"So what do I do? What do I do about Rick? About Mama and Daddy and our home? About my job here and maybe going up to work with Aunt Lillian? What should I eat when I get home? That last one was a joke. Mama made a pecan pie last night that's calling my name. But I'm serious about the rest of it. What should I do?"

She brushed the grass growing beneath the headstone. Six feet below where she was sitting was a wooden box with her brother inside. No, not her brother. Just his body. Josh was with God in heaven. He may not have been an A+ kid and he got into some trouble that he shouldn't have, but Serenity knew that he had been saved by God's grace. She could see the love of Christ in him when he would talk to people or help someone who was down on their luck. Hanging out with the wrong crowd didn't cancel that out.

At that moment, Serenity felt something stir in her soul, and she heard her brother's voice speak inside her.

Don't ask me. I'm not here anymore. Ask God.

It was so obvious, Serenity felt embarrassed, even though there was no one else around. Here she was, talking to a cold, lifeless headstone, when the Almighty God who formed her with His own hands was watching her and loving her at that moment, and for all eternity. And He was always listening.

"God," Serenity said, sniffling back her sorrow, "I feel so lost right now. Please help me. Please."

She hugged her legs and rested her head on her knees. She wasn't expecting an angel to descend with a scroll containing detailed instructions for her life. She wasn't even expecting an answer right now. It was nice to just be quiet and know that she had asked the Person who had the answers. One of Mama's favorite verses came to mind, in 1 Peter 5:7: *"Cast all your anxiety on Him because He cares for you."*

Even just praying made her feel better. The answers would come. Right now, she was just going to spend some quiet time with her brother.

****

"...And bless this food to the nourishment of our bodies. Amen."

"Amen."

"Amen."

Serenity opened her eyes and immediately started helping herself to green bean casserole. She could feel her mother's gaze on her but she purposefully avoided making eye contact.

Greg grabbed a pork chop and passed the platter. "So how was your day, sweetheart?"

Serenity put a pork chop on her plate and handed the platter to her mother. Patti's eyes locked with hers for a second and she looked away.

"It was, uh, not bad, really," Serenity stammered. She began cutting into the meat with furious strokes.

Greg looked at her suspiciously and then at Patti, who pursed her lips and put her hand on Serenity's arm.

"Tell us," she said quietly.

Serenity's knife stopped mid–slice. She stared at a spot on the tablecloth for a moment and then set down her cutlery.

"I went to see him today. Rick, out at his uncle's place."

"His uncle's place?" Greg said with a frown. "His uncle ain't lived there for ages. Died, I think."

"His uncle died and he inherited the land. He's fixing up the old farmhouse. He wants to sell the property. I reckon once he does that, he'll be moving on."

"That's what he meant when he said he won't be around long," Patti said to no one in particular. She looked at Serenity with a gentle smile. "How was it, talking with him again?"

"Hard to say," Serenity said. That wasn't exactly the truth but she wasn't about to spill the beans about everything at the dinner table. "He told me about his life since he went away. He was in the Marines and got deployed over in Afghanistan. Sounds like he had some pretty rough times over there. And he also told me that he's a born–again believer now."

Greg's eyebrows flew up. "What now?"

"He said he got saved while he was over there and he's been walking with the Lord ever since. Surprised me too when he said it. I never should have been with him back then, and not just because of Josh. I was just a stupid girl who got swept off her feet. I knew y'all didn't approve and I knew it wasn't wise for a Christian girl like me to be with a non–Christian boy. If I had been a little smarter then, things would be a whole lot different."

"Come now," Patti said, giving her hand a squeeze. "No more boo–hooing and living in the past. We can't change what we've done or what's been done to us. What we can do is try to make the future as right as we can. Which is why – "

She smoothed out her napkin on her lap and gave her husband a resilient look that was still twinged with hesitation.

"– I called Pastor Avery and told him to reach out to Rick to invite him to supper tomorrow evening."

"Mama!"

"Patti, are you sure?"

"Yes," Patti declared, helping herself to some mashed potatoes with her chin slightly elevated. She carried herself this way whenever she'd made a decision that she knew might not be popular but she wasn't going to budge for anyone or anything. "He's made the first step and now we're going to meet him halfway. The Bible tells us not to hold a grudge, especially not against another believer, if what he says is true. We all need this. Y'all know I'm right."

Greg chewed thoughtfully on a piece of meat. "Yeah, I suppose we do. Don't know what I'll say to him, though."

"I think it's best we just listen, anyway. What do you think, sweetheart? It's going to be uncomfortable for all of us, but this is something we have to do as a family."

Serenity swallowed hard. Her throat felt like sandpaper. "I guess so. But I ain't going to lie, I really think we should wait a bit. Maybe give him time to think about what he'd like to say to us."

"He's had plenty of time to think, sweetheart. I'm sure he knows what he wants to say."

Serenity gave her a half-hearted smile and quietly finished her food. After helping Mama with the dishes, she went up to her room. She wasn't ready to go to bed but she didn't want to be around people right now. There were some new episodes of a show she liked on Netflix but she didn't feel like watching TV either. After taking a shower and changing into her pajamas, she sat down at her desk and turned on her computer. There was one thing she never got tired of, and that was watching horse videos on YouTube. She followed a channel that belonged to a famous horse trainer and there were new videos every week. Serenity watched the latest one, taking note of how the trainer used pressure with the stick to control an ornery horse. The trainer also gave tips on how to teach beginner riders, which Serenity always found helpful. She had been doing her own lessons for a couple years now, but she knew there was still so much to learn. With some of the kids dropping out of her class, it made her even more motivated to step up her game and be the best trainer she could possibly be.

A small voice piped up in the back of her head. *If you went up to stay with Aunt Lillian, you could get a first-hand education. That would open a lot of doors.*

It definitely would. But Aunt Lillian lived six hundred miles away in Nebraska. Serenity was needed here. How would her parents survive with both children gone?

You wouldn't be dead, silly. And that's why they have video chat.

Serenity rolled her eyes and told the little voice to shut up. She wasn't going to Aunt Lillian's and that was that.

But there was still the question of money. What could she do to boost her classes?

She spun around in her desk chair a few times, then grabbed her phone off her pillow. She pulled up Kelly's number and dialed it.

"Hello?" Kelly answered.

"Hey, Kelly."

"Hey, Serenity. Listen, I'm sorry about the dance. I didn't mean to ditch you like that. And I'm sorry about Chris. I feel like such an idiot. I thought he was into me but he told me he was going to Houston to be near his wife and kids. Why did I even think he was an option for me? I'm so stupid. I got sick after the dance so he took me home and I was in bed for a couple days, and then when I go to the pharmacy to get some medicine, I see him driving off with a fake blonde bimbo who was certainly not his wife. What a jerk. I should have blown him off and hung out with you instead."

Serenity blinked a couple of times, trying to process the avalanche of words. "It's okay, Kelly. We all make mistakes. Speaking of which, you know Rick Stevens is back in town, right?"

"Yeah, I heard. Have you talked to him yet?"

"Sort of." Serenity paused, considering how much she should tell her. "I'm going to see him again soon. Anyway, that's not why I called."

"What's up?"

"How close are you to the principal?"

"Mr. Brady? I don't know... I'm just a teacher's assistant. But I think he likes me. As a teacher, I mean. I've chatted with him a few times, and I think I'll get a full–time job there once I finish my early childhood education degree. Why?"

"Well, I wanted to see if it would be possible to bring a horse to school."

Kelly's voice had a smile.

"What did you have in mind?"

****

Serenity's eyes were on the seven–year–old girl on top of Jasmine and her hands were holding the lead line in a firm grip, but her mind was in another place. Another time, actually. Tonight, to be specific. Pastor Avery had called Mama this morning to confirm that Rick was coming over for supper at six o'clock. The pastor had asked if the family wanted him present as well but Mama told him that they needed to do this on their own, and he had agreed.

It wasn't until the lesson was over and the little girl had been picked up by her parents, who thankfully confirmed that they would like to continue her lessons through the spring, that she realized she had been clenching her stomach muscles all morning. She was starting to feel a bit of a cramp, and after riding Jasmine around the pasture for a few minutes to let the horse burn off some energy, she took her back to her stall and then leaned against the trunk of the tree outside the barn. Deep breath in, deep breath out. A few more times, and she could feel the tension start to ebb.

She hated feeling like this. She was used to being laid back, relaxed, enjoying every day with her family and horses. And now, things were getting a little too real too fast. Serenity wasn't naïve but she knew she had lived a relatively sheltered life. Aside from Josh's passing, she and her family had never experienced any serious crises. The twisters that came through twelve years ago were about the biggest drama she'd ever encountered, even though the storm only tore off part of the roof. Some folks lost everything. She had always wondered what that must have felt like, to lose your home, and how inconceivable it was to her back then. And now, she was afraid that she was going to find out first-hand.

She raised her head and stared out across the undulating grass.

That's it. She was *afraid*. Afraid of her family losing their home. Afraid of having no place to keep her beloved horses. Afraid of leaving all of this behind and going to a strange place to live and work. Afraid of having dinner tonight with Rick.

This wasn't her. She wasn't a fearful person. She may not have had a twister come and shatter her house to pieces, but she'd been battered and broken enough, and she'd always picked herself up again.

She was going to do the same thing this time. She wasn't going to sulk or cry or get a stomach cramp. She was going to take the reins. If she could control these massive animals, she could control her future. And she sure as heck wasn't going to lose it in front of Rick like she did the other day.

Why did her life have to come to a halt just because he was back in town? The sun was still shining, the wind was still blowing. Life was still happening, as it always did. He was just a tumbleweed that was blowing on through. You don't crash your car because a tumbleweed finds its way onto the road. You watch it roll on by and you keep driving.

Serenity took off her hat and slapped the dust off her leg. She knew what she was going to do. She was going to go inside, get cleaned up, and help Mama prepare supper. She wanted to see Rick's face when he tried her muffins. She was going to show him that she was doing just fine and dandy without him.

She was going to let him say what he wanted to say, and then she was going to show him the door.

Cool, fresh air filled her lungs as she marched up toward the house. Now she was actually looking forward to tonight.

CHAPTER TEN

PATTI FINISHED setting out the silverware and stepped back to take in the table arrangement.

"Well, that's that," she declared.

Serenity nodded her approval. "I think I knew the proper place setting for every plate, cup, knife, spoon, and fork before I could cook anything by myself."

"No daughter of mine is going to grow up without proper domestic management skills," Patti said, stabbing the air with her finger.

"You know how many women would cringe to hear you say that?"

"Let them cringe. There ain't no shame in a woman taking care of her house and family when that's her choice to do so. And there *is* shame in letting her house and family fall apart when she's out there chasing fame and fortune. Call me old-fashioned, but when I read

Proverbs 31, I see a woman who is strong, independent, and responsible. People can say what they want, but I find a great deal of joy and satisfaction in a home–cooked meal and a nice table presentation."

"Amen."

The two women stood silent for a moment, admiring their handiwork. Then Patti turned to her daughter.

"I feel a little nervous."

Serenity gave her what she hoped was an encouraging smile. Her defiant attitude from the afternoon was starting to wilt, and if she was being honest with herself, she would have to admit that she was nervous too. "It'll be okay, Mama," she said, putting her head on her mother's shoulder. Nothing more needed to be said; they both knew what was in each other's hearts.

The sounds of tires crunching on gravel and headlights sweeping through the window grabbed their attention. Serenity immediately recognized those heavy footsteps on the front porch.

"Hi, Daddy," she said when Greg came in.

"Hi, darling," he answered, leaning down to kiss her cheek. He gave Patti a peck as well and nodded his approval when he saw the table spread.

"Looks great, and smells delicious."

Patti helped him take off his jacket. "Nice day at work?" she asked. Usually small talk waited until supper but everyone knew there wouldn't be much time for that tonight.

"Yep. Sold two of them new Marlins. I just been finishing up getting everything together for the trip this weekend. Still need to get some new coveralls, though. I don't have any in my size at the store."

"That might be a challenge no matter where you go, Daddy," Serenity said with a grin.

"Are you saying that I'm too tall?"

"Yes, that's exactly what I'm saying. You're too tall."

Greg gave her a knowing smile and pulled his girls close. He gave them each a kiss on the top of the head.

"Y'all ready for tonight?"

Patti smoothed out her apron. "As ready as we'll ever be. Serenity made poppy seed muffins."

Greg licked his lips. "Well, no matter how tonight goes, at least we'll have some good eatin'."

Right on cue, another car pulled up. Serenity looked at Patti.

"I'll go out and meet him."

"Are you sure?"

"Yes."

She squeezed her mother's hand and opened the front door. The sky was fading into twilight, casting a soft rose glow over everything, including Rick as he got out of his red late-model Chevy pickup truck. Serenity's eyebrows rose a bit when she noticed the vehicle. It must have cost a pretty penny.

Rick was bending over to get something from the back seat when Serenity came out of the house. She stopped, stared for a moment, then reluctantly forced her eyes to look off to the side.

"Howdy, Serenity."

She snapped her head back around, hoping she wasn't blushing.

"Hi, Rick."

He held out a bouquet of roses. "Before you say anything, I just want to tell you how sorry I am that I upset you the other day. It was selfish of me to just unload on you like that. I know me coming here was your mama's idea, but if you want me to leave, I'll get right back in my truck and get out of your hair."

Serenity cradled the flowers, savoring their mesmerizing color. She let Rick's question hang in the air for a few suspenseful moments, then shook her head.

"It's all right. I shouldn't have overreacted like that. Things have just been pretty stressful in my life recently, aside from you showing up. But it's good that you're here. My folks are eager to talk to you."

Be strong and aloof. Let him know you don't care one way or the other.

Serenity cleared her throat. "You know Mama. She's so traditional and polite. Even if you were a stranger, she'd invite you to supper. Daddy's been super busy. I'm surprised he made it home in time. This was all last minute for all of us, really. You're lucky we had the time to get together."

"Oh," Rick said. "I suppose I am lucky."

Serenity nodded, then realized after a few seconds that she was still nodding. She stopped her head's movement with an abrupt flinch, startling Rick. To hide her embarrassment, Serenity turned around and gestured toward the house with the bouquet.

"Well, get on in there. Supper's getting cold."

She couldn't see his face because her back was turned but she knew he was smiling.

"Yes ma'am," he said, walking up the steps ahead of her and opening the door. He swept his hand inside. "After you."

She gave him a cold glance, lifted her chin, and strode into the house. He came in behind her and closed the door. Patti and Greg were standing in the foyer in front of the stairs. They stared at Rick, and he stared back. Serenity took it upon herself to break the ice.

"Mama, Daddy, Rick is here."

Rick offered his hand to Greg. "Thank y'all for inviting me over. I know it's not easy, me being here."

Greg looked at Rick's hand for a long moment, then reached out and embraced him in a crushing bear hug. Patti joined in the embrace. Serenity stood off to the side, holding the flowers, her mouth hanging slack like a playground swing.

Someone started crying. Serenity couldn't be sure, but it sounded like Daddy. The whimpers lasted for just a moment, though. Greg hastily broke away and wiped his eyes. Patti was crying too but she didn't mind if people saw. Serenity thought she also saw Rick's eyes sparkle.

She was too perplexed to move. Did she really just see that?

"Oh, what lovely flowers." Patti took the roses from her and went into the kitchen to fetch a vase.

Rick looked back at Serenity. He was just as puzzled as she was. He turned to Greg with a grateful smile. "That's not at all the welcome I expected."

Beets curled around his legs and purred happily. Rick looked down at the cat and smiled in surprise.

Greg put his hand on Rick's shoulder. "Tell you the truth, I didn't know what I'd do or say when you arrived. But I know the healing power of forgiveness, and the thing about forgiveness is, it's unconditional. You can't say, 'Well, if they do this or that...' It's all in. And I want you to know is that we forgive you. Right here and now, without any conditions. I want us to start on the right foot."

Rick looked like he was going to cry again. "Thank you, sir."

"We still want to hear you out," Patti said, returning with the flowers gracefully arranged in a light blue vase. "We know you have lots of things to get off your chest. But first comes supper."

"Lead the way."

Greg led Rick into the kitchen with Patti following behind. Serenity stood alone in the foyer, still paralyzed with shock.

Patti stuck her head out. "Sweetheart, let's eat."

Serenity's limbs felt numb as she forced herself to walk into the kitchen. She passed the counter and sat down at the table across from Rick. He was sitting in Josh's old seat.

Greg held out his hands. Serenity took his left hand and Rick took his right. Rick offered his hand to Patti, who offered hers to Serenity. When the circle was complete, Greg bowed his head.

"Dear Lord in Heaven, thank You for bringing Rick to us tonight. Thank You for bringing him into Your family, and thank You for loving us and forgiving us while we were still sinners. Bless our time tonight, bless this food, and bless the hands that prepared it. In Your Son's name, amen."

"Amen," Rick and Patti echoed.

"Amen," Serenity whispered.

Greg handed Rick a platter of roast beef. "Dig in."

Rick happily obliged, and after the dishes had circulated, everyone's plates were piled high with food. For the first few minutes, no one spoke. Rick ate like he hadn't had a decent meal in days, which was probably the truth. Patti was positively glowing. Greg was too absorbed in his own plate to notice. Serenity picked at her food, hardly tasting it. She watched every move Rick made as if he might suddenly fling his chair back and bolt out of the house. Or maybe that's what *she* wanted to do.

What in the world was going on here?

"So Rick," Patti said, taking a sip of sweet tea, "Serenity tells us that you got saved over there in Pakistan."

"Mama," Serenity snapped.

"It's all right," Rick said, his mouth still full of poppy seed muffin. After swallowing, he continued. "Afghanistan, ma'am. And yes, the Lord laid His hand on me out there in the desert. At first, it might have been just from a fear of dying, but soon I could feel a real change in my heart. My buddies noticed it too. I was a good soldier but always had kind of a bad attitude. When God got a hold of my heart, all that went away. I was still scared, and I still fought for my country, but I knew that no matter what man did to my body, my soul was safe with God in Heaven."

"Well, amen to that," Greg said, raising his glass in a toast. Rick and Patti raised theirs. Serenity followed numbly, taking the smallest sip of tasteless tea.

"Honey, are you all right?" Patti asked.

"Yes Mama, I'm fine."

"You've barely eaten anything."

"I'm fine, Mama."

"All right." Patti took another bite of fried okra, looking unconvinced. But she didn't press the issue.

"We're glad you made it back in one piece, Rick," Greg said. "I know plenty didn't."

"Yes, sir." Rick stared at his glass of sweet tea. "Plenty didn't."

Serenity cleared her throat. Despite this very weird evening, she wasn't going to be the black sheep.

"Rick's fixing up his uncle's place out on 441," she said, perhaps a bit too loudly.

"Oh, is that right?" Patti said, feigning surprise. "How is that going?"

"It's hard, ma'am. The place is in quite a state."

"I can imagine," Greg said. "How long has it been laying empty?"

"A couple years. My uncle passed on while I was deployed and no one in my family wanted it. When I came back, it sort of fell in my lap."

"So what's your plan?"

"Well, fix it up, get it presentable, and then search out a buyer."

"And then what?"

"Greg!" Patti hissed.

"I'm just asking the boy. It ain't an interrogation, just an honest question."

"I don't mind, ma'am," Rick said, throwing a cautious glance toward Serenity. She sipped her tea, keeping her eyes on his. He blinked, then turned to Greg. "Honestly sir, I ain't thought that far ahead. I saved a good chunk of my salary while I was over there.

Plus, I'm still enlisted in the Reserves. I report to base down in Forth Worth once a month. My time in the service has taught me to get by on little. Heck, my phone is just a twenty dollar burner from Walmart."

"You know anything about computers?"

Rick glanced at Patti and Serenity. "Uh, I know a thing or two."

"Think you might be able to help me set up a website for my store?"

"Daddy! This is dinner, not a job interview."

Greg pointed at Rick with his muffin. "Just think about it."

"Yes, sir." Rick lowered his head and worked on his food. Serenity got the impression that he was deliberately avoiding making eye contact with her.

Thankfully, the rest of the meal passed in silence. Serenity was still trying to wrap her head around what was going on with her folks. Rick was a charmer, she had to give him that. Those warm green eyes would melt any heart. She did her best to choke down her food to avoid arousing Mama's worry, but she hardly tasted a bite. Too many thoughts and feelings were swirling around in her head. Part of her was glad that the night had started on such a positive note, but she wasn't sure she was so ready to offer him her forgiveness like her parents had. It was as if they had completely forgotten he was the reason Josh had gone out that night and never come home.

Patti, Greg, and Rick seemed to finish their food almost at the same time. Rick leaned back in his chair and patted his stomach.

"That was unbelievable, Mrs. MacAlister." He fixed his eyes on Serenity. "And thank you, Serenity. I know those were your poppy seed muffins."

Her cheeks felt warm. "Thank you," she said quietly.

"Dessert?" Patti asked hopefully.

Rick waved his hands. "I couldn't hold another bite, ma'am, but thank you. Maybe after my food has settled a bit."

He looked at each of them in turn, and the expression on his face indicated that the night was about to take a serious turn.

"If y'all don't mind, I'd like to say what I came here to say."

Greg looked at Patti. "Sure," he said, rising to his feet. "Let's go to the living room."

"I'll brew some coffee," Patti said.

Serenity followed Greg into the living room. He settled into his chair and Serenity and Rick sat on opposite ends of the sofa. Rick patted the cushions.

"I remember this furniture," he said with a grin. "Softest cushions I ever sat on."

"Glad to hear it," Patti said as she entered the room. She sat down on the edge of the love seat. "Coffee will be ready in a few."

"Thank you, ma'am."

Rick looked at Serenity for a long moment. She wished more

than anything she could know what he was thinking. He took a deep breath, folded his hands, and leaned forward.

"Y'all really caught me off guard when I got here. That was the nicest welcome anyone's ever given me, and if anyone has reason to give me the cold shoulder, it's y'all. I deeply appreciate it from the bottom of my heart."

"So do we," Patti said.

"Thank you, ma'am." Rick took another deep breath. "I apologize for the ambush at church. I've been a nervous wreck since I been here. I wanted to talk to y'all and the Aggers and the Conways but I wasn't sure how to go about it. I didn't want to be all sneaky because I didn't want to hurt people's feelings that I came to this family or that family first, so I figured I'd just broadcast myself for all to see. I'm sincerely sorry if I shook y'all up."

"You showing up like that was a bit of a shock," Greg said. "But we understand why you did it that way."

"I hope so. And I meant what I said, that I wanted to talk to everyone I'd hurt and see if there was any way I could make amends. I know I can never bring Josh back, but if it's all right with you, I want to tell y'all my side of things, and whatever y'all decide after that, I'll be at your mercy."

Greg looked at his wife and daughter. "Fair enough."

"Thank you, sir." Rick cleared his throat. "First of all, I want to apologize to you, Serenity. I was a bad boyfriend. Not in a cheating sort of way, but I was just not the right person to be in a relationship with a girl as amazing as you were back then, and still are. I was reckless and stupid and a bad influence. I know y'all didn't approve of me dating your daughter," he said to Greg and Patti, "and it was wrong of me not to respect your wishes. Your daughter is your treasure and it wasn't my place to take her away without your blessing."

Greg's face was stern but he nodded slowly. "I'm glad to hear you say that, Rick."

"Yes," Patti agreed. She reached out and took Serenity's hand. "She is our treasure."

"Which is why it's hard for me to say this," Rick added.

Serenity's heart fell into her stomach.

"The night of the accident," Rick continued, staring at the coffee table in front of him, "I was with Serenity, as y'all know. And I was...trying to go a little farther than was appropriate. She didn't agree, and I was disappointed. That's why I brought her home early that night. And on the way, Josh texted me that he had heard about this party down by the river, and I told him that I was on the way here anyway, so that's why he went with me."

His expression changed. His mouth twitched and then he buried his face in his hands. A tear fell from between his fingers.

Greg and Patti sat like statues, watching Rick sob on their sofa. Serenity's mouth hung open as her eyes searched the floor.

Going to the party was Josh's idea, not Rick's. All this time, she had blamed Rick for taking Josh out that night, when in reality, it was Josh who wanted to go.

Serenity felt like her heart was imploding inside her chest. She looked at Rick, saw his shoulders tremble as he wept into his hands. Part of her wanted to reach out and comfort him, and the other part wanted to strangle him.

Rick looked up, his face streaked with tears. "I'm so sorry," he said to Serenity. "I'm sorry for the way I treated you, and I'm sorry for not taking better care of your brother that night. I shouldn't have let him drive my truck. I should have been the responsible one. Three good guys died that night and I'm the only one who walked out of that wreck, and I should have been the one to go." His hand touched the scar on his cheek. "Every night, I ask God why. Every morning, I wake up without a clear answer. I just hope that my life means something."

He paused and wiped his nose. "I understand if y'all never want to see me again. But I had to get it all out, let you know all of it. Please don't be angry at Serenity; put it all on me. I was the scumbag. I didn't deserve your daughter back then, and I don't deserve your hospitality now. I'll just go."

Rick rose to his feet.

"Sit down!" Greg bellowed.

Serenity flinched and watched Rick slowly sit back down on

the sofa. He looked like he had just stumbled into a lion's cage.

Greg fixed him with his fierce blue eyes. "You got a lot of courage, boy, coming into my house and telling me about you getting fresh with my daughter and admitting your failures as a friend to Josh. Yes, you should have been more responsible. Yes, you should have had his back. Yes, you young bucks shouldn't have even been drinking that night, or any night. You should have been at home studying for a math test or reading *The Warrior Ethos*. Might have done you a heap of good. But what's done is done, and nothing can change it, even spilling your guts like this. Now here's the thing about forgiveness, son – it don't matter if you come into some more information about the situation. There ain't no conditions or clauses or takebacks. I forgave you the moment you walked into this house, and that hasn't changed because of what you've just told us. And the only way I can forgive you is because I know that I was forgiven even while I still hated God. It don't mean I ain't mad, and I miss my son every moment of every day, but you didn't kill him. And even though you played a part in the accident, it wasn't your fault. So I don't want you carrying around a burden of guilt that ain't yours to bear. You survived that crash for a reason. There are no accidents in God's plan."

Rick looked like he was going to burst into tears again.

Even though every cell in her body screamed, *'What are you doing?!'* Serenity reached across the sofa and put her hand on his back. He felt so warm. He gave her a thankful smile and looked down at his wet hands.

"I don't know what to say to y'all. I can't thank you enough, Mr. MacAlister. You have no idea what your words mean to me. Mrs. MacAlister, I know how much you loved your son. I would gladly trade my life for his. But since God has seen fit to keep me here, I want you to know that I will do anything that you think would help the pain. Work, money, anything."

Patti gave a quick nod. She was struggling to hold back her tears as well. "Thank you, Rick."

Rick looked at Serenity again. "I'm sorry for everything I took from you. I don't even deserve to be in the same room as you. But if there is anything I can do for you, anything at all, I'm at your service anytime."

Serenity held his gaze, trying to push through the whirlwind of emotions. "Okay."

Rick took a deep breath and held his hands open. "That's all I have to say, really. Is there anything y'all want to ask me or tell me?"

Greg looked at the ladies, then rose from his chair.

"I think that's enough for tonight. We've all got a lot to process. But we meant every word we said. And we'd like to have you back here one day."

Rick glanced at Patti, who confirmed her husband's offer with a nod. "You don't know how much this means to us, Rick," she said.

"I can't tell y'all how nervous I was coming over here," Rick said as he stood up. "I ain't under no illusions that everything is honky-dory between us, but I want to become someone that you are glad to know, instead of someone who brings up bad memories."

"Time and the Lord will help with that," Patti said, giving him a gentle embrace. Greg stuck out his hand and Rick shook it gladly. "Serenity," Patti added, "would you please see our guest out to his car?"

Serenity looked intently at her mother's face, trying to ascertain her reasons. "Yes, Mama," she agreed. "I'll see you out, Mr. Stevens."

Rick smiled. "Thank you, Miss MacAlister."

He nodded to her parents and followed her outside. The stars were beautiful in the velvet sky, and the songs of the crickets and frogs pierced the cool night air. The two of them walked in silence to Rick's truck.

"I'm sorry, too," Serenity blurted when he opened the door. Rick stopped and looked at her with a confused expression.

"Sorry for what?"

Serenity looked at her boots, which were barely visible in the dark. "I'm sorry for holding onto my anger against you. I'm still mad; I suppose I'll always be mad. But it ain't right to put it on you. All this time, I'd been thinking it was your idea to go to that party down by the river. That don't let you off the hook, but it gives me one less reason to hate you."

Rick gave her a smirk. "Gee, thanks."

"You know what I mean."

"I do. And you're right. The fact remains that some stupid kids did some stupid things, and they paid the price and I got away with just this scar on my face. They talked about 'survivor's guilt' in the military and it's a real thing. Men died under my command, and I have to live with that for the rest of my life. But the guilt and regret I feel about Josh being gone is greater than any pain I feel about those soldiers losing their lives on my watch. It all hurts, though, and that ain't never going away. It's part of who I am now. But more importantly, I've found God's forgiveness, and if you and your folks can forgive me the way y'all did, it shows me more than ever that the love of Christ is real."

Serenity dug her toe in the dirt. She wanted to tell him that she was still wrestling with her own guilt, that she wasn't sure she had forgiven him yet, that there were times that she was furious at God for what had happened to her family. But all she could do was shrug.

"I suppose. We ain't saints, though. We're just regular folks trying to pick up the pieces."

"Ain't we all. Listen..."

Serenity's heart froze. *Please don't say something that will make this more awkward than it already is.*

"...I know this wasn't easy for you. And I'm sure you probably had half a mind to rip my head off. Maybe you still do. But I can see how strong you are inside, like your folks. You come from good stock."

Serenity didn't know what to say. She could only brush away her hair out of her eyes and murmur, "Thanks."

Rick looked at the open truck door. "Well, I best be going. Good night, Serenity."

"Good night, Rick."

She stepped back as he started the truck. He gave her a sweet smile tinged with melancholy before he drove off into the night. Serenity watched his taillights disappear, feeling like her heart was breaking all over again.

He said you're strong. Be strong!

Serenity hugged herself against the cool night air as she walked back toward the house.

When she came back inside, Patti and Greg were clearing the table. Patti set down her plate and opened her arms.

"Come here, sweetheart."

Serenity melted into her embrace. Greg surrounded both of them with his big arms, and for a few happy moments, they existed in the warm shelter of each other's love.

"You okay?" Patti asked softly.

"Mm-hmm," Serenity said, taking a step back. "Y'all really surprised me."

Patti and Greg traded weary smiles. "We surprised ourselves,"

Greg said. "Something just came over me as soon as that boy walked into the house. It was almost like I heard God speaking in my heart, telling me that this was the chance to show what it truly means to be a child of God. Forgiveness can be one of the hardest things to do but also one of the easiest. And doggone if it don't feel good."

"Amen," Patti added.

Serenity looked at both of them like they were crazy. Then she threw up their hands. "I guess I still have a lot to learn."

"We all do," Patti said, giving her one more quick hug. "Now let's get this place cleaned up. Oh darn! I forgot the coffee."

An hour later, after the dishes had been put in the dishwasher and the table wiped down and the floor swept, Serenity sat in her dark room, staring out the window. She could just barely see the curve of the low hills in the distance. There was only a sliver of a moon tonight, and the stars were big and bright. A meteorite zipped across the sky, seeming to disappear into the trees on the horizon.

Her stomach was still tight, as it had been all evening. She played with her fingers, bending the joints forward and backward the way she often did when she was nervous or upset. There were so many feelings wrestling with one another in her heart, she didn't know which one was winning.

One thing she did know, though. There was still anger in there, including at God, but especially against herself and against Rick. It's one thing to *say* that you forgive someone, but it's another thing to really mean it.

She knew it was the right thing to do. She also knew that the only way she would find the strength to forgive was if she prayed about it.

But she couldn't. Something held her back. She could only stare out the window into the endless night sky.

CHAPTER ELEVEN

THE NEXT FEW DAYS WERE quite busy, and Serenity was grateful for the distractions. Running here, running there, doing errands, tending to a sick Crack Shot, and helping Mama pick out decorations for the church's Thanksgiving supper in a few weeks helped keep her mind off of Rick.

Well, most of the time, anyway.

She and her parents didn't talk about that fateful evening again, though Serenity got the impression that Mama did want to bring it up but was making a concerted effort to avoid the subject. Daddy was busy at the shop, and tomorrow, he was heading out with three of his longtime buddies to Oklahoma for a bowhunting trip. He always came back with at least one whitetail in the cooler, and Serenity was looking forward to Mama's legendary venison chili.

Crack Shot wasn't ailing too bad, just an autumn cold, but Serenity never liked to see her horses feel uncomfortable. Jasmine and Hillbilly also seemed upset. They would shuffle around their stalls in agitation whenever she came around to check on him. She picked up some medicine from the vet but that set her back a couple hundred dollars, money that she needed for a new kids' saddle. Her old one was falling apart, and she had gotten it well-used in the first place, and she needed to be able to keep the kids safe. She knew she had to stay positive, but things weren't looking so good right now.

Then on a cold, rainy night, she got a call from Kelly.

She held the phone up to her ear and said, "Hello?"

"The principal said 'yes'!"

Serenity frowned, trying to figure ou–

"Oh my gosh!"

She leaped off of her bed and did a fist pump in the air.

"Thank you, Kelly! Thank you thank you thank you!"

"You're welcome, girl. I'm stoked too."

Serenity flopped back down on the bed and looked up at the ceiling.

"I don't know why I didn't think of this sooner. I'm kind of nervous now, actually."

"You'll be great! What kids don't love horses?"

"You'd be surprised."

"Well, even if they don't love horses, they'll love *you*. And so will their folks."

Serenity took a deep breath. She knew she was grinning like an idiot.

"Thanks, Kelly. You're awesome. This is such a big help to me."

"Anytime, sugar. Oh, the principal said they can only do this Friday."

"That's in three days!"

"Yeah, I know. Sorry, I wish they had given me more advance notice. Can you make it work?"

"I think so," Serenity said, chewing on her bottom lip. Her heart was pounding like a freight train.

"Come on, girl, you're a beast. You got this."

"You're right. I got this."

"Do you think you can put a flier together and send it to me in an email? I can print it out and put it in the kids' folders tomorrow."

Serenity glanced at her computer. "Um, yeah, I think so. Just don't laugh, okay?"

"I won't. At least not to your face."

"Ugh. Well, I'll get right on it."

"Okay. Love you, babe."

"Love you too."

Serenity hung up and stared at the wall. Doing a live training demo in front of the students and their parents was going to be scary. But if she wanted to drum up some business, she had to show them the goods.

She jumped into her desk chair and brought her computer to life. Time to put those Microsoft Paint skills to work.

****

"You sure you going to be okay, sweetheart?"

Serenity helped Mama into her coat and patted her face like she was a child.

"I'll be fine, Mama. I've transported horses by myself before. Besides, what could you do to help me, anyway?"

Patti shrugged. "Moral support."

"You can give that to me from the doctor's office. Your appointment is in two hours and you don't want to take the chance of getting stuck behind a tractor and being late."

"Okay, okay." Patti's eyes sparkled. "Look at you. My, my, my. I pass your baby picture on the wall on the stairs every day, and then I look at you now, all grown up like this. It breaks my heart and fills me with joy at the same time."

"Oh, Mama, don't get all soft on me now. Go on, out you go before you start crying or something."

Serenity gave her a gentle shove but Patti spun around and squeezed her tight.

"Good luck today, sweetheart. Be careful."

"I will, Mama." Serenity pushed her away. "Now go!"

"I'm going." Patti opened the door, stepped one foot out, then turned around again. "Think your father's bagged anything yet?"

"*Go!*"

Patti jumped as if Serenity had thrown a firecracker at her feet. She hurried down the steps, got into her bright red Mazda, and drove off, waving her hand out the window. Serenity watched her from the front porch, hands on her hips. *Bless her heart...*

If she was being honest with herself, though, it would be nice to have Daddy around. Loading up a horse and hitching the trailer to a truck was easier with two sets of eyes and two pairs of hands. Serenity had actually never done it completely by herself – she just told Mama that so she wouldn't worry. But still, she knew she could handle it.

The demo was at 11 o'clock so she had an hour and a half to get ready, load up, and get down to the school. She already had her cutest cowgirl clothes on, and she'd even tied her hair in the ribbon from the Harvest Dance. Butterflies were bouncing off the walls of her stomach, but she was also really excited. She had gone to school at Jonesburg Elementary as a child and it was nice to think of how she'd come full circle.

A bird chirped urgently from the trees. Serenity got the message. No more dilly–dallying.

After checking the mirror once more and gathering her bundle of promotional materials that she had hastily printed out at the UPS store in town yesterday, she hopped in the truck and went to the barn. She drove around to the back where the trailer sat. It was an old rust bucket but it was always reliable. At least it had been the last time it was used, which was almost a year ago. Serenity backed up to within a couple of feet and got out to raise the coupler and line up the ball with the socket.

She looked down. Her heart fell to her feet.

The right tire was as flat as a popped balloon.

Serenity slapped her legs and ground her teeth. Of course. Why wouldn't the tire be flat when she was in a hurry and all by herself?

She checked her phone. An hour and twenty minutes. If she got the tire changed in fifteen minutes, she would have plenty of time to load up Jasmine and her gear and get down to the school with time to set up.

Frustration boiled underneath her skin and she clenched her fists. She let out one angry snarl, inhaled, exhaled, and then ran back up the hill to the house. She knew that Daddy kept the jack and tire iron in the shed. When she was halfway there, she thought that maybe she should have checked the spare tire next to the fender to see if it was in working condition before rushing up here. Her fury burned hot again. It was too late to do anything about it. She'd get the jack and tire iron and then pray that the spare was usable.

Pray. That's another thing she forgot.

"Lord," she said out loud, panting as she hurried up the hill, "please help me get this sorted out. I ain't in no mood today and I'd appreciate a hand if You don't mind."

A breeze tickled her face, cooling her warm cheeks. It felt good and her heart brightened a bit. She made it to the shed and threw the doors open wide. A dozen musty and oily smells slammed into her nose but she didn't have time to gag. She remembered seeing the jack behind the tool box back some months ago and she prayed that it was still there.

Praise the Lord, it was, along with the tire iron. They were heavy and dirty but that was irrelevant. Right now, she needed to hightail it back down to the barn and get that tire changed.

Hurrying down the packed dirt path, she mentally reviewed the steps for changing a tire in her mind. She had only changed one by herself, and that was a couple of years ago. Where did the jack go for lifting a trailer? She assumed there would be a groove on the frame but if not, she'd just put it close to the axle. A trailer was a lot lighter than a car, anyway. Shouldn't take too much effort to lift it.

Doubts swooped through her mind like howling demons. She clenched her jaw and marched down the hill with a strong, measured stride.

You can do this. Just a flat tire.

She was just starting to believe herself when she reached the back of the barn and saw the hopelessly deflated tire again, and her confidence deflated along with it. Dropping the jack and tire iron, she went over to the left side of the trailer to squeeze the spare. It was fully inflated, and her heart sang. One hurdle conquered...

She crouched down next to the flat as best as she could without putting her knees on the ground. She didn't want to mess up her jeans, but she quickly realized that she wouldn't be able to get a look under the trailer without getting down on all fours. Groaning in annoyance, she gingerly placed her knees on the cleanest, driest patch of ground she found and leaned down for a look under the trailer. She saw the groove in the frame where the jack would fit in, and her confidence jumped up another notch.

See? You got this.

She slid the jack under the frame and connected the jack rod. After several hard pumps, she got the flat lifted off the ground. One more hurdle. All she had to do was get this wheel off, detach the spare, and bolt it on. She fitted the tire iron over the first nut and gave it a tug.

It didn't budge.

She strained and grunted, turning as hard to the left as she could. Not even a millimeter of movement. Serenity blew her hair out of her eyes and tried a different nut. Same thing. The nut didn't look terribly rusted but it wasn't in the best of shape either. She tried each nut and couldn't turn a single one.

The sun beat down on her back, which was already streaked with sweat despite the breeze. She squinted up at the bright sky.

"Please, Lord. I need to get this tire off."

She paused, as if waiting for some sort of sign. Then she realized she was wasting valuable time. She put every ounce of strength she had into that tire iron, twisting until the veins popped in her forehead.

Those nuts were going nowhere.

She flung the tire iron down in disgust and fell heavily against the trailer. It wobbled but stayed on the jack. Serenity felt the tears starting to well up but she commanded them to stay put. She wasn't going to cry like a little princess. She was stronger than that.

But she also wasn't getting this wheel off, either. And if she couldn't get it off, then she wasn't going to make it to the school.

She pressed her hands to her face, then quickly pulled them away, hoping she hadn't smudged her makeup. Why did Daddy have to be on his hunting trip? Why couldn't it have been last week, or next week?

Serenity pulled out her phone and opened her contacts. She scrolled through the names, which was actually a pretty short list. No one except Pastor Avery would be able to help her, and she knew that he visited the nursing home in Pelton on Fridays. She looked up at the sky again, struggling with all her might to hold back the tears.

A name popped into her head. Her shoulders slumped.

No. Nuh-uh. No way.

She watched in horror as her thumb pressed the call logs and found Rick's number.

Do not call him. Do. Not. Call. Him.

A sigh of exasperation escaped her lips. She hoped God was

enjoying His little joke.

She pressed "Call," cringed, and held the phone to her ear. After three rings, Rick picked up.

"Hello?"

Another pause. "Hey Rick, it's Serenity."

"Hi, Serenity. How's it going?"

"Great. Look, I don't have time to chat, so I'll just get to it. I need your help changing the tire on my horse trailer."

"Oh. Okay. No problem. I'm actually in town, just picked up some things from the hardware store. I can be there in ten minutes."

"Great. I'm behind the barn. See you then."

She hung up and groaned again. She had sounded so rude. Not even a "thank you." If she were him, she wouldn't even show up.

She hoped he wasn't like her.

After giving the nuts a few more hopeless tries, she kicked the flat tire, trying to keep bad words out of her mind. She had less than an hour to get to the school. So instead of sitting around feeling frustrated, she went into the tack room in the barn and brought out the saddle, bridle, food, and water. As she was bringing Jasmine out, Rick pulled up in his truck. Serenity watched him get out, noticing that he had the same dirty sleeveless t-shirt from the day she had gone over to his place. Surely it wasn't the same one... Well, either way, his muscular arms were on full display. A thought popped into Serenity's head before she could swat it away: *if those arms can't get those nuts loose, then nothing can.*

"Hey."

Serenity realized she was staring and jerked her head up. "Hey," she blurted, inadvertently tugging on Jasmine's reins. The horse blustered and nudged her arm.

Rick smiled. "So what's up?"

It was killing her to be the damsel in distress, so she tried to play it cool.

"Tire's flat and the nuts won't budge," she said casually, pointing at the trailer. "Gave it my best shot but guess they're rusted on nice and good."

Rick bent down to take a look. "Hmm, don't see too much rust."

He picked up the tire iron and fitted it onto a nut. As she watched him strain and grimace, a part of her wished that he wouldn't be able to get it off either. That was crazy, of course, but she felt so humiliated by having to call him out here, it would give her a small amount of perverse satisfaction if he also failed.

The nut gave a squeak and Rick lurched forward.

"There we go," he announced victoriously, spinning the tire iron and pulling off the nut. "Here."

He slapped the nut into her hand before she could do anything. He didn't notice her incredulous glare as he went to work on the other nuts. In two minutes, he had the wheel off, then went around the trailer to take off the spare. Serenity looked at the lug nuts in her hand and listened to Rick's grunts coming from the other side of the trailer. A soft breeze stroked her face, and an even softer voice spoke in her heart.

See? I will always take care of you.

Serenity looked at Jasmine and shook her head. Yeah, but did God's provision have to manifest itself like this?

Rick emerged from the other side of the trailer holding the spare tire against his chest. He squatted down and fitted the wheel on the bolts.

"Where you off to?" he asked as he held out his hand.

Serenity dropped a lug nut into his palm and cocked her hips. "The elementary school."

Rick tightened the nut and held out his hand again. "What for?"

"A demo for the kids and their parents. Hopefully going to get some new customers."

"Sounds great. What time is your show?"

Serenity closed her eyes. "Thirty minutes," she said through clenched teeth.

Rick looked over his shoulder at her, his eyes wide. "Thirty minutes? You're not even hitched up yet!"

"I know, Rick!" she snapped. "I wasn't planning on having a flat tire today!"

Rick held up his hands. "All right, all right. I'm sorry, didn't mean to upset you." He took a deep breath. "Listen, let me get this wheel on and lower the jack. You load up the horse and I'll hitch your truck to the trailer."

"No, you don't need to – "

"Yes, I do. You want to be late for your show and give people a bad impression?"

Serenity glared down at him, then looked away. "Okay." Her nostrils flared, and she added, "Thanks."

Rick gave her an infuriating grin. "No problem. Happy to help a damsel in distress."

"Hey now, listen, I'm not – "

"I was talking about Jasmine."

Serenity's eye shot daggers, and he quickly turned back around to finish bolting on the wheel. After the nuts were in place, he pumped the jack rod and lowered the trailer.

"All right, load her up," he said, wiping his hands on his shirt. "Keys in the truck?"

Serenity nodded. Rick went around to the front of the trailer and started raising the coupler. Before she loaded Jasmine inside, Serenity glanced at him over her shoulder. Despite her mixed feelings, she was glad he was here.

She guided Jasmine inside and bolted the door shut, then reached through the window and stroked the horse's nose.

"Just a short ride, girl. Take it easy back there."

Jasmine nibbled on her hand. Serenity smiled, then watched as Rick eased the truck back, placing the trailer hitch ball perfectly under the coupler. He jumped out, gave her a wink, and rapidly lowered the coupler until the full weight of the trailer rested on the ball.

"Good to go," he declared. Serenity could tell that he was proud of himself. She nodded her appreciation.

"Thanks."

He glanced at his watch, then narrowed his eyes at her. Serenity's heart stopped. She knew what he was going to ask.

"Listen," he said after clearing his throat, "you'll probably say no, but if you like, I can go with you and help you set up. You ain't going to make it with more than a minute or two to spare and I imagine you'll be needing to talk to folks and begin your demonstration right away. I can unload everything while you're doing that. I know my way around horses."

Serenity was so furious, she wanted to pop. But he was right. Doggone it, why was he right?

"Okay, fine. But you look like you just changed a tire."

Rick looked down at his dirty shirt. "Oh, I got a clean shirt in my truck. Be right back."

He dashed off to his truck and opened the back door. His back was turned to her as he peeled off his sleeveless t-shirt. Her heart fluttered and her cheeks flushed with heat. The time in the military had certainly done him some good...

After buttoning up his brown–and–white flannel shirt, he threw the dirty shirt into the back seat of his truck and got in the driver's seat.

"I'll follow you," he called out as he turned over the truck's engine.

Serenity glared at him and got into her truck. She shifted the truck into drive and started easing down the gravel driveway, checking the rearview mirror to make sure Jasmine was okay. Rick followed close behind in his truck.

She turned her attention in front of her, feeling moisture underneath her palms.

God, what are You doing?

CHAPTER TWELVE

KELLY RAN UP to the truck as it pulled out onto the field beside the elementary school.

"Serenity!" she sputtered breathlessly as she practically slammed into the driver's side door when Serenity rolled down the window. "Where have you been? We're just about to – "

She saw Rick pull up alongside her. She looked at Serenity. Serenity drew her lips in a line.

"Long story."

Kelly gave her a raised–eyebrows look that had a dozen meanings, then she pulled open the door. "Get on out there! People are waiting for you!"

Rick got out and came around. "I'll saddle up Jasmine and bring her over to you."

"You sure you can handle it? She doesn't know you."

"Trust me," Rick said with a beaming smile. "Horses love me."

Serenity's stomach twisted in fear but she knew she didn't have a choice. *Please don't let Jasmine get spooked in front of all these people.* "Okay. Just walk her over to me nice and easy."

"You got it."

He went to the back of the trailer to unlock the door. Kelly grabbed Serenity's arm and leaned in close.

"Not now," Serenity hissed as they headed toward the rickety bleachers. They were on the school's backup soccer field, which was good for little more than getting soggy in the rain and occasionally hosting school activities. Serenity scanned the faces and figured maybe two dozen kids and about a dozen parents. If she could convert just three of those kids into paying students...

Kelly pulled her toward a bald man in a checkered sweater vest.

"Serenity, this is Principal Brady."

He offered his hand and she shook it warmly.

"Thank you so much for having me here, sir," she said with a bright smile. Today was all about winning people over.

Principal Brady returned the smile. "My pleasure, young lady. It's nice to have an activity like this just before Friday lunch. Routine is good but we need to mix it up sometimes. Where's your horse?"

Serenity glanced over her shoulder. Rick was gently easing Jasmine out of the trailer. He was right – the horse did look relaxed. "My, uh, assistant is getting her ready and will bring her over in just a minute."

Principal Brady clapped his hands. "Ah, great. Why don't you introduce yourself to the kids and their folks in the meantime?"

Kelly gave her an encouraging look. Serenity nodded.

"Sure. Let's get this show on the road."

Principal Brady looked relieved as he escorted the girls over to the bleachers. Kelly let go of Serenity's arm and stood off to the side, giving her a thumbs–up.

Serenity hoped she didn't look nervous. All eyes were on her. A hundred doubts swirled through her mind: Did her hair look okay? Were her clothes clean? Did anyone notice the dusty spots on her knees? Should she have worn a different hat? Did she remember to close the zipper on her jeans? Did she –

The fliers and sign–up sheet. She had left them in the truck.

Catching herself just before she winced, she gave everyone a perky smile and a wave.

"Howdy, y'all!"

"Howdy," several people responded. Many of the kids, especially the girls, were paying keen attention. So were most of the parents, especially the handful of fathers.

Time to work the magic.

She opened her mouth, froze for a moment, then smiled again. "I'm Serenity Hope MacAlister," she said, finally finding her voice. "I'm sure a few of you know me. My daddy runs Mr. Mac's Hunting and Fishing Supplies over off of West and Main, and my mama has her hands in just about everyone's business in town."

A few people snickered, knowing that she was right.

Their laughter was encouraging. "First I want to thank y'all for coming out," she continued. "I know y'all parents have got a million other things to do, and y'all kids probably have some exciting math problems to do, right?"

"Nooo!" the children shrieked. More laughter from the parents.

"Well, I won't keep y'all for too long. I just wanted to show y'all a beautiful horse named Jasmine and teach you a thing or two about riding. How many of you know how to ride a horse?"

Several of the parents and three kids raised their hands.

Good. The parents were the first hurdle.

"How many of y'all have ever ridden a horse before, even once?" she asked the kids.

Most of the children raised their hands. "At the fair," one boy said.

"My auntie has horses," another declared.

"That's good," Serenity replied. "I love horses. My job is teaching kids like you how to ride, but most importantly, how to love horses as much as I do. And you know what?"

"What?" several asked.

"The horses love you right back."

"Like a doggie?" a little girl with missing front teeth piped up.

"Even more," Serenity said with a smile. "Plus, a horse is a pet that you can ride! Can you ride on a doggie?"

The children giggled, and then their eyes opened wide and their mouths fell open. Everyone turned to their right, and Serenity followed their gaze.

Rick rode high on the saddle, holding the reins in a bunch with one hand. He was grinning from ear to ear as Jasmine trotted briskly across the field. He reined her in a few yards from Serenity and looked at the eager crowd.

"Howdy, y'all!"

"Howdy!" everyone replied.

He dismounted in one smooth motion and led Jasmine over to Serenity, handing her the reins. Serenity took them, staring at him in surprise. He gave her a wink, then turned to the crowd with a flourish.

"Ain't she a beauty?" he asked with a sweep of his arms. "And the horse ain't bad-looking, either!"

The parents laughed. Serenity could see the mothers' sparkling eyes.

Rick patted Jasmine's flank. "I'm Rick, and I'm a friend of Miss Serenity's, and I can tell you that she is one of the most gifted horse trainers I know, and I've met quite a few. But the best part is that she loves kids just as much as she loves horses, which is pretty rare. You usually only get one or the other. Today y'all are in for a treat, because she is going to show you just how special these animals can be."

He stepped aside and the audience gave him some brief applause. Serenity was still staring at him and holding Jasmine's reins. Her heart skipped a beat when he reached behind his back and pulled out a roll of papers from his belt. He gave her a look that said, *"You're on!"* and she turned to the kids and their parents.

"Thanks, Rick. He'll pass around some fliers for y'all along with a sign-up sheet if you're interested in lessons or just want to know more about me and what I do. I ain't super big on social media but I have some photos and information on Facebook and Instagram if y'all want to check that out. All right, who wants to see some riding?"

Every hand went up. Serenity gave Rick a grateful smile before she mounted the saddle. Rick handed fliers to the parents and then stood off to the side and watched.

Serenity and Jasmine took off across the field in a gallop. Excitement pulsed in her veins as the breeze rushed across her face. She turned Jasmine hard and raced back to the bleachers, pulling Jasmine back so the horse reared back on her hind legs. The children gasped and clapped their hands.

For the next half hour, she demonstrated her capabilities as a trainer and a teacher, leading Jasmine, having her walk backwards, follow behind her, even nibble on her hat. The children howled and watched with keen attention, and the parents seemed to be entertained as well. Serenity led Jasmine over to the kids and let them touch her nose. Then she asked if anyone would like to sit on the horse. Almost every child raised their hand. Serenity selected a little girl whose mother was in attendance and gave her approval. The girl had clearly been around horses before but she still showed some slight hesitation when Serenity hoisted her up on the saddle. Keeping a firm grip on the reins, Serenity guided Jasmine around an invisible arena, telling the girl what to do to make her stop, go, or turn. Jasmine responded perfectly to every command. The kids were mesmerized. Even Principal Brady looked delighted. Kelly and Rick were standing on opposite sides of the bleachers and each gave her smiles of encouragement.

When her time was up, Serenity thanked everyone for sharing a little part of their day with her, and she reminded the parents to contact her if they had any questions. She also told the children to bring the fliers back home to their parents who weren't there today and to tell them how much they enjoyed watching the lady with the horse. Many children came up and hugged her and petted Serenity once more. Principal Brady gave his phone to Kelly and asked her to take a picture of the three of them. He said the photo would go on the school's website and would be published in the monthly newsletter that went home with students. Serenity thanked him again for letting her do this demonstration.

"Anytime," he said, shaking her hand once more. He also

offered his hand to Rick. "That was quite an entrance, young man."

"Thank you, sir," Rick said.

The principal pointed at both of them. "You two make a good team. I'm sure you'll be hearing from some of the parents and kids here today. Best of luck!"

Before Serenity could correct him, he turned and motioned for Kelly to follow. Kelly put her hand up to her ear and mouthed "Call me!" Serenity nodded, catching Kelly's sly smile.

She turned to Rick. "Thanks for your help," she said. "I couldn't have done this without you."

"No sweat." He shielded his eyes from the sun as he looked across the field. "Let's pack it in, then."

Serenity pulled on Jasmine's reins as they walked back to the truck.

"I had fun," Rick said, keeping his eyes on the grass.

"Me too."

A pause. "Do you think people think we're a – "

"Team?" Serenity interrupted.

Rick grinned. "Yeah, a team. I hope people don't think I'm part of the teaching staff."

"I think those moms would be disappointed if they find out you aren't. By the way, where did that come from? I hardly ever saw you ride when we were younger."

"I rode some," Rick said with a shrug. "Never had a horse of my own, just up at my uncle's place. Don't take this the wrong way, but I used to think horses were kind of a chick thing. When you got your first horse – Hillbilly, right? – I thought about asking you to go riding but I was wanting to be all cool and macho, so I didn't talk about it. Stupid, huh?"

"Yes, really stupid. That's about the dumbest thing I ever heard."

"I know. And I felt kind of bad about it after we broke up and I went off to basic. As fate would have it, after I got deployed to Afghanistan, my unit was stationed close to a village that had a reputation as being a good place for horse breeding. In the spirit of 'winning hearts and minds,' I became a ranch hand of sorts when I wasn't on patrol. Nothing like what you were doing, just tending to the horses, riding them around for exercise, stuff like that. The horses weren't anything you'd see at the Kentucky Derby or nothing, but they were still pretty fine animals."

Serenity looked at him with an expression of half–amusement, half–surprise. She shook her head and laughed sharply.

"Wow. Rick Stevens goes off to fight the Taliban and comes back knowing how to ride horses."

Rick shrugged again. "Funny world, ain't it?"

"Yeah."

They fell silent again. A circling hawk screeched.

Rick looked at her with one eye shut to the sun. "You, uh, want to go get something to eat?"

Serenity chewed on her bottom lip for a moment. "Some other time, Rick."

He nodded and looked off to the side. "Well, let me help you load up."

After Jasmine and the gear were secured in the back of the trailer, Serenity stuck out her hand.

"Thanks again for helping me today."

Rick shook her hand. "Happy to help. I hope you catch some new fish for your school."

Serenity squinted at him, then her face brightened with understanding. "Ah, good one. He's got jokes."

"You have no idea."

He let go of her hand and went over to his truck. Just as he was about to get in, Serenity called out, "Hey."

He turned around. Serenity stared off into the distance for a few seconds, then tapped the hood of her truck.

"You want to come over and ride sometime?"

Rick grinned. "You bet. Just give me a call. You know where I'll be."

Serenity watched him drive off, closing her eyes when the cloud of dust washed over her. The hawk overhead screeched again, and Jasmine brayed from the trailer.

"All right, all right, hold your – "

She chuckled and got in the truck. She had jokes too.

****

Greg came home the next night, and it was nice to have him back. Serenity didn't tell him about the flat tire. Her parents apparently hadn't heard about Rick's knight-in-shining-armor rescue and she wanted to keep it that way. Kelly also hadn't called her to ask for the scoop, at least not yet.

She lay in bed, staring up at the dark ceiling. There used to be glow-in-the-dark stars up there when she was a kid. She had the stars and Josh had the planets. A sweet sadness gripped her heart and she rolled over so she could see the family picture by her bedside. It was taken on a fishing trip about four months before Josh died.

Serenity reached out and touched the glass. They all looked so happy. Josh was proudly displaying a smallmouth bass that he had caught. Actually, Daddy had to help him reel it in, but Josh was so excited, his smile about split his face in half.

That's how she liked to remember him. Always smiling, always carefree. A bit of a scamp, a bit of a troublemaker, but with a heart of gold. They had their fights, like all siblings do, but they always had each other's backs. And they had plenty of adventures that Mama and Daddy would never know about.

Serenity smiled as a tear spilled out of her eye and disappeared into the pillow fabric.

"Miss you, bro," she whispered, touching his picture. She sniffled back the remaining tears and turned over on her back again. Maybe she should put those stars back up there...

Like a meteorite streaking across the sky, Rick's face flashed through her mind for the dozenth time today. She grit her teeth and shut her eyes, trying to force him out of her thoughts. It was futile, of course. She let out a sigh and decided that instead of fighting it, she was going to let him percolate in her head for a little while.

It was looking more and more likely that he had turned out all right. She wondered if he had attracted attention from other women in town. Maybe some of the single moms at the school today were going to try their luck. Maybe he was on a date with one of them right now...

Yeah, right. She pulled the plug on that ludicrous train of thought and let her thoughts circle back around to him. His soft green eyes still made her heart flutter, but there was something more that made them even more appealing. Maturity, perhaps? World–weariness? Sorrow? Guilt? The right sunlight? Whatever it was, she could look into them all day. And those muscles... She felt her face become warm and she tried to divert her thoughts elsewhere, but she couldn't help letting her mind's eye linger for a bit. His strength when he fought that flat tire, and the way he controlled Jasmine... She'd always felt like "sexy" was kind of a dirty word but she couldn't deny that it suited him.

Okay, enough about the outside. She took a few quick breaths and told her imagination to calm down. Handsome men were a dime a dozen (not really, but she had to tell herself *something*). What really matters is the heart. This was where she saw the biggest change in him. He seemed more gentle, perhaps even meek, despite his strength. Was that a direct result of him coming to Christ? The cocky, arrogant swagger was gone, replaced by a gentle strength that she saw in good Christian men like Daddy and Pastor Avery. It defied logic that someone like Rick with a chip on his shoulder would go into the military and come out more humble than when he went in. Yet she could see it, plain as day. His strength had increased but his pride had receded. Something like that only happens when God gets a hold of someone's heart.

It was hard for her to admit, but she was glad he was back. She frowned. Glad? How about just "intrigued" or "pleasantly surprised"? She searched her heart. No, she was glad. Glad that he had changed, glad that he had come back for what seemed like honorable reasons, and glad that she and her family had a chance to reconcile with him.

So what now?

She looked over at the family picture. Josh smiled back. She raised her eyes and looked out the window, at the real stars twinkling in the night sky.

There was certainly no easy answer for this one.

CHAPTER THIRTEEN

ON THE WAY TO CHURCH the next morning, Serenity wondered if Rick would be there too. It would certainly be a lot less awkward if he wasn't. But deep down, she knew she would be disappointed.

Her parents hadn't mentioned him at all since the emotional dinner several days ago. Mama was her usual inscrutable self, the picture of southern charm and grace with something simmering just below the surface. Daddy's hunting trip seemed to do him a lot of good. He'd been upbeat and chipper ever since he got back. She even noticed him holding Mama's hand a couple of times.

When they got to church, Serenity searched the faces of the congregation, hoping she'd spot Rick and also wishing she wouldn't. Ugh, these feelings were so annoying! It was like being in high school again.

She told her parents that she was going to the bathroom. It was true that she needed to go, but she mostly wanted an excuse to scan as much of the sanctuary as possible. She made her way slowly through the aisles and went to the ladies' room. When she came back out, the worship band was up front, getting ready to start the morning songs. Serenity looked around one last time, then sulked back to where her parents were sitting.

There was someone else with them.

"Hi, honey," Patti said when Serenity sat down next to her. "Look who we saw."

Rick waved cheerily. Serenity waved back.

"I hope it's all right that we asked him to sit with us," Patti whispered.

Serenity nodded quickly, hoping Rick hadn't heard her mother. "It's fine, Mama." She glanced at Rick again, who was still smiling.

If the sermon was about anything to do with relationships, she was going to walk right out of the church.

Fortunately, the message was about Paul's letter to the Galatians where he talks about the fruits of the Spirit. As Pastor Avery went through the list – love, joy, peace, patience, kindness, goodness faithfulness, gentleness, self–control – Serenity realized how little these virtues were evident in her own life. Her thoughts centered around anxiety, guilt, hastiness, and insecurity. When the pastor concluded the message with a prayer, she offered her own words up to God.

Lord, please let the fruits of Your Spirit shine in my life. My name is Serenity but I hardly feel any peace these days. Please calm my anxious heart and let me rest in Your strength and plan for my life.

When she raised her head, she felt like she had been cleansed in cool, refreshing water. Life wasn't going to become perfect with the snap of a finger, but God was in control of it all. No matter what happens, no matter how crazy life seems, God is always in control, and it is foolish to think that anyone knows better than He does.

After the service, Pastor Avery made his way over to them. He shook Greg's hand, then Rick's.

"I'm so happy to see y'all together," he said, his face beaming. "This is the picture of God's church right here." He gave Serenity a knowing smile. "I heard that y'all two put on quite a show for them youngsters over at the elementary school."

Patti looked at her daughter with an expression that said, *"Oh, really?"*

Serenity tried to smile but it came out more as a smirk. *"Tell you about it later."*

Patti's haughty eyes said, *"You better."*

She turned to Rick and touched his arm. "Rick, would you like to come over for lunch? I fear that you must be eating some frightful food every day out there by yourself. Do you even have running water and electricity?"

Rick laughed. "Yes ma'am, I do. Though you're right; most of my meals are cooked in the microwave or on the grill."

Patti pressed her hand to her chest. "Oh Lord have mercy."

"Now don't fret, dear," Greg interjected. "There's a certain simple charm about the bachelor's life and eating habits."

"Would you like to go back to those days?"

"No," Greg said to his shoes.

Patti raised her nose in victory. "Rick, it is the judgment of this court that you are in dire need of a good home-cooked meal."

"I thank you, ma'am, I really do, but I already have an appointment that I must keep."

Serenity's eyebrows rose. Maybe one of the school moms *were* bold enough...

"We'll take a rain check," Patti said. "Man does not live on microwaved ramen alone."

"I did," Greg murmured.

"What's that?"

"Nothing."

Rick looked at his watch. "So sorry to turn down your kind invitation, ma'am. And I'd love to take that rain check." He shook Greg's hand and nodded to Serenity. "Have a nice day, Serenity."

They watched him leave the church, and then Patti looked at her daughter. "Do you mind telling us what Pastor Avery was talking about?"

Serenity suppressed a groan. "I'll tell you in the car."

****

She filled them in on the way home, keeping the details to a minimum and repeatedly mentioning how it was no big deal. Even though she couldn't see her mother's face, Serenity could picture her terse expression. Greg apologized for not being there to help her, explaining that he should have checked on those tires a while ago. Serenity assured him that it wasn't his fault, and that she needed to learn how to handle herself sometimes. He reminded her that she had to call Rick to bail her out. She didn't say anything back.

Lunch was simple but delicious – Reuben sandwiches with Swiss cheese on toasted bread rolls and mac n' cheese on the side. And of course, homemade sweet tea. After everything was cleaned up, Patti announced that she was going upstairs for a nap. Greg was going to do some tinkering on his truck. Serenity had to pick up a few things in town and volunteered to get some groceries as well. Greg told her that she didn't have to do that, but Serenity insisted. Patti gave her a grateful smile.

The early November wind was crisp and cool but the sunshine was still warm, making it a perfect day to drive with the windows down. The radio played upbeat country songs as Serenity sped down the road, feeling joy in her heart as she bobbed her head and sang along. It always amazed her what a little prayer could do.

First stop was picking up some feed for the horses. When the truck was loaded up, she headed on over to the grocery store, using the list she had grabbed from the refrigerator. It took nearly all the cash she had on hand to buy everything, but this was her responsibility too. Anxiety about her family's future started creeping into her thoughts but she silenced them with Philippians 4:6 – *"Be anxious for nothing, but in everything by prayer and supplication, with thanksgiving, let your requests be made known to God."* Instantly, her thoughts became calm. She had to smile. There really was power in God's Word.

When she came out of the grocery store, she glanced at the diner across the street. Was that Rick's truck in the parking lot? This was Texas and there were a lot of trucks around, but that shade of red...

She looked up at the diner and gasped.

Rick was sitting in the window seat.

Her heart skipped a beat and she flattened herself against her own truck, still holding the grocery bags. He hadn't seen her, but that was because he wasn't eating alone. Sitting across from him was a blonde-haired woman. At this distance, she couldn't tell if the woman was his age or older, but Serenity could at least see that she was pretty. They were both eating and talking, and from the woman's body language and the way she was leaning forward, she was very interested in what Rick had to say.

Serenity's fists tightened around the handles of the grocery bags. Rick had blown off Mama's invitation to a home-cooked meal so he could – what? Go on a date? At a *diner?*

There were a dozen other explanations, Serenity knew. The woman could be an old friend, or a family member, or even a former teacher. She *did* look a little bit like Serenity's tenth grade social studies teacher, Miss Hammond. She was only in her mid-twenties then and all the boys had crushes on her.

Serenity squinted. No, that wasn't Miss Hammond. So who *was* she, and why in the world was Rick having lunch with her on a Sunday afternoon?

She nearly yelped when she saw them get up from their seats. Her grocery bags jostled together as she fumbled with the truck door handle, yanking it open and flinging herself inside just as Rick and the mystery woman came outside. She peeked over the back seat, hoping that Rick wouldn't notice her truck parked across the street.

He didn't notice because he was too busy smiling and chatting with the blonde. Serenity studied her carefully, taking note of her athletic figure, her confident, hip-swinging walk, her fashionable clothes, and her dazzling smile.

Serenity gasped. She knew why that woman looked so familiar. She was one of the mothers at the school on Friday. She had been perched on the top bleacher, sitting a little ways apart from everyone else.

A dark shadow passed over Serenity's face. This blonde looked like the kind of woman who was used to getting what she wanted, and Rick had fallen for it hook, line, and sinker.

And now they were getting in Rick's truck together! Serenity couldn't believe what she was seeing. Rick was all smiles, jabbering away, and the woman laughed as they drove off in the direction of Rick's place. Serenity's eyes followed the truck until it turned a corner and disappeared.

She looked down at her hands. That joy she was feeling before? All gone.

This is stupid, she told herself. *You're being stupid. He's not yours. He can hang out with whoever he wants. And you don't know what you saw, anyway.*

It didn't matter. She saw enough.

Maybe she should follow them. Not too close, just enough to see where they were going. What if they were going back to his place? No, Rick wouldn't do that. He was a changed man, a decent man.

He's been back in town for just a few weeks. You don't know nearly as much as you think you do.

She squeezed her eyes shut and clenched her teeth. Why was she such an idiot?

She shifted into reverse and backed out of the parking space. Forget him. Let him do what he wants. He wants to play around with women ten years older than him? Fine. She drove through town, heading back to her home. The radio bleated a dreary song about lost love and she angrily turned it off.

But what if it's not what you think and you're wasting your chance?

Wasting her chance for what? A second chance at a relationship? With *Rick Stevens?* The guy who had been a bad influence on her when they were dating? The guy who was with her brother when he died? The guy who disappeared for four years and then waltzed back into town like a cowboy in a Western movie?

Yes.

Serenity pressed her lips together and growled in her throat. *Doggone it...*

She grabbed her phone from her pocket and dialed Rick's number. She pressed the phone to her ear with her shoulder as she kept both hands on the wheel.

On the fourth ring, Rick answered.

"Hello?"

"Hey Rick, it's Serenity."

"Hi, Serenity. What's up?"

"You busy?"

"Nope. You need help with something? Got another flat?"

The only thing flat was Serenity's voice. "No. I wanted to see if you had some free time tomorrow afternoon to go for a little ride."

A pause. "Yeah, sure. That would be nice."

"Great. See you at two o'clock."

She hung up and dropped the phone on the passenger car seat. Her heart was pounding so loudly in her chest, she could feel her shirt move. She rolled down the window to let the cool breeze blow on her face. Her cheeks were hot enough to melt right off.

She tried to think of something else, anything else, besides Rick in his truck with that beautiful blonde. Frustrated, she slapped the radio back on. The song was energetic and chipper, and she sang along loudly, hoping it would help.

It didn't.

CHAPTER FOURTEEN

THE NEXT DAY, Serenity had Crack Shot and Jasmine saddled up and bridled at ten minutes 'til two. She grabbed the reins and brought the horses outside, shielding her eyes from the sun as she stared across the grass. She stood there and waited, checking her phone every couple of minutes.

1:56.

1:58.

At 1:59, she spotted Rick's truck crawling up the driveway toward the barn. She wrinkled her nose and flared her nostrils. She was hoping that he would be late so she could have a good reason to be annoyed at him. He parked the truck and got out, smiling at her as if he hadn't gone out with a blonde soccer mom yesterday afternoon.

"Howdy," he said when he walked up.

"Howdy. Right on time."

"The military will make you punctual."

"Hmm."

She handed him Crack Shot's reins. He looked confused.

"I thought you said that Jasmine likes me."

"She does. And you should know by now that when a girl likes a guy, she always plays hard to get."

Rick raised an eyebrow. "Does she now?"

Serenity turned up her nose and hoisted herself up onto Jasmine's back. She was using the saddle that she used for her kids for their lessons since Rick would need the bigger saddle for Crack Shot. The cinch on the kid's saddle was wearing out and the tree seemed to have a bit more give than normal but she figured it would be all right for an afternoon ride. "Get on up there," she commanded him.

"Uhh..." Rick looked at Crack Shot with concern. "This guy seems a bit skittish. Will he be all right with a new rider?"

"He usually is. Ain't tossed anyone in a while."

"Uh-huh."

Rick stroked the horse's nose and rubbed his shoulder. Serenity sat on Jasmine and watched. She didn't really want Crack Shot to give him a hard time but she would be at least a little amused if he did.

Holding the reins tight, Rick mounted the saddle and pulled Crack Shot's head to the right. That wasn't particularly where he wanted to go but he showed Crack Shot his strength and dominance, and the horse seemed to get the message. Crack Shot shook his mane and shuffled his hooves but otherwise, he was completely docile.

Serenity pursed her lips. "Looks like you really did learn a thing or two out there in the desert."

"It was grassland, mostly. Some hills too. Kind of like here."

"So my family's home is comparable to Afghanistan."

Rick laughed. "That's not what I meant."

"Huh. Less talk, more riding."

Rick spoke up as she turned Jasmine around. "Shouldn't we get some water or something?"

Serenity patted the saddle bags. "Mama made some snacks too."

"Oh."

"She's probably watching us from the house right now."

Rick craned his neck to look at the house over the crest of the hill. Serenity gave the reins a light snap and Jasmine began trotting through the grass.

"Let's see what you got, slowpoke!" Serenity called over her shoulder.

Rick eased his horse forward, careful to not spook the animal. Crack Shot wasn't in the mood for cautious emotional bonding and he started after Serenity and Jasmine at a brisk trot. He leaned his head forward, pulling at the reins just enough to let Rick know that he wanted to hit the gas. Rick grinned and gave him a strong squeeze with his heels.

Serenity heard the pounding hoofbeats and looked behind her. Rick and Crack Shot were only half a dozen yards back. She gave Rick a challenging smile and leaned down close to Jasmine's ear.

"Let's show these boys how it's done."

Jasmine snorted and charged forward at Serenity's urging. Rick saw her speed away and he snapped the reins.

"Let's get 'em, boy!"

The horses and their riders galloped across the grass, down into the valleys and charging up the hills. Serenity looked over her left shoulder and was startled when she didn't see Rick.

"Yoo–hoo."

She turned to her right and saw him right next to her. Crack Shot was neck and neck with Jasmine. Serenity stuck out her tongue and darted ahead. Rick's hearty laugh rang out across the hills as he raced after her.

For several minutes, they galloped through the grass, zig-zagging across the property since the land size wasn't big enough for them to make a straight line across for more than a minute. Serenity and Jasmine stayed out in front most of the time, but just as they approached the grove of trees at the corner of the property, Rick leaned Crack Shot in close. Jasmine instinctively broke away, losing a bit on the trajectory. Rick darted in front, reaching the trees just before Serenity pulled up behind him.

"You cheated," she accused with a pointed finger.

Rick smile innocently. "Just a little race track strategy. You could have done the same to me at any time."

"I'm not as devious as you."

"I suppose not." Rick dismounted and held out his hand. "Help you down?"

Serenity looked at his hand in contempt. "No thanks. I'm a big girl."

"Yes, you are."

Her eyes flashed with fire. "What?"

Rick's face turned red. "I mean that you're not little. I mean...you're not a little girl, you're...big..."

He cowered beneath her glare. Serenity knew good and well what he meant, but sometimes it was just so fun to mess with guys. It was all she could do to hold her fearsome expression and watch Rick cringe like a kid about to get spanked. She let the terror linger for a moment, then swung her leg over Jasmine's back.

The cinch beneath Jasmine's belly broke with a *snap!* Serenity yelped as she fell back...right into Rick's arms. The saddle plummeted to the ground and Jasmine trotted off in a huff.

Serenity and Rick were motionless. He held her with his strong arms as if she were light as a feather. Her hands were around his shoulders, and she could feel his warmth through his shirt. They stared into each other's eyes, their lips only one breath apart.

Serenity's heart thundered in her chest, and she could feel his heart beating against her.

Everything rushed over her in a wave – the sweet memories of young love, the yearning for him when he was gone, the joy and anger at his return. She watched his lips, wondering if maybe...

He cleared his throat and set her on her feet. Serenity quickly turned aside, brushing her hair out of her eyes. She knelt down next to the saddle and lifted it up to look underneath. The tree was cracked in a nice jagged line. It would cause any horse tremendous discomfort, not to mention the fact that the cinch that held it in place was snapped in half.

"Doggone it!" She put her hands on her hips and kicked the useless saddle.

Rick bent down and examined the cinch. "Wow, lucky that didn't happen while you were riding. That would have certainly ruined your day."

Serenity's heart was still pounding, and she looked up at Jasmine, who was grazing with Crack Shot.

"Yeah, guess you're right. But that was the saddle I use for my classes. The one on Crack Shot is a little too big for the kids."

"Well, it'll have to do," Rick said as he stood up. "For now, at least."

Serenity looked at him. "What do you mean?"

Rick shrugged. "Nothing."

Serenity smirked. "Thirsty?"

"Yep."

She knelt down and dug out two water bottles from the saddle bags and also grabbed a sandwich bag with some jerky that Mama had packed. They went over to one of the trees and sat down. Rick thanked her and tore into a strip of meat, then took a long gulp of water. Serenity watched him with narrowed eyes.

"How was your appointment yesterday?"

Rick wiped his mouth. "Fine. Just working on something."

"Something?"

He looked at her with a guilty expression. "Yeah. Might be something, might be nothing. We'll see."

"Hmm."

"What, 'hmm'?"

"Nothing."

Rick held her gaze for a moment and took another bite of jerky.

"Why'd you ask me to come riding with you?"

Serenity looked up at the red-tinted leaves. "Why not?"

"That's not an answer."

A bird chirped high up in the branches. Serenity searched for it, then lowered her eyes.

"It's just nice not to be alone sometimes."

"How can you be alone? You have great parents and beautiful

horses."

"That's not what I meant."

Rick looked out across the grass. "I know. Me too. I thought that coming back here would feel like home again but it's so different. Almost everything is the same since when I left, so I guess it's me that's changed. Of course, not having my family here is also a big part."

"Where are they again?"

"My dad lives near El Paso and my mom and sisters are up in Colorado where my grandma lives."

"When did your folks split? Was it because of the accident?"

Rick shook his head. "No, things were rocky way before that. It might have been the final wedge, though. I remember getting a handwritten letter from my mom while I was at basic. For some reason, reading it in her handwriting made it hurt worse than if she had called or even shown up in person. I saw them once before I got deployed, a couple times on holiday leave, and I visited her and my sisters before I came down here after I got discharged. I ain't seen my dad yet. Kind of got to work myself up to that one."

Serenity could see the melancholy in his eyes. "I'm sorry," she said.

He shrugged, trying to maintain a tough face. "No family's perfect, even when they look like it on the outside. I suppose that's why I was the way I was and I am the way I am. But now that I know that God has forgiven me, I've been able to forgive them."

He looked at her cautiously.

"Have you decided if you can forgive me or not?"

Serenity sighed and hugged her knees. "Come on, Rick. Do we have to talk about this now? Can't we just enjoy a pleasant afternoon with the sunshine and the horses?"

"Okay." Rick took another bite of jerky.

Several long, heavy moments passed. Serenity swatted a fly away in frustration.

"Yes," she snapped, deliberately avoiding his eyes. "I forgive you. Don't mean I ain't still mad or sad sometimes though."

"Thank you," Rick said with a smile. Serenity had the feeling that he wanted to say more but he fell silent and chewed on his jerky.

"This is where Josh and me used to play," Serenity said, looking up at the branches.

"Josh told me. He and I came out here one time with a couple airplane bottles of Jack."

Serenity threw him a sour look. Rick held up his hands.

"Hey, his idea. Don't make it right, of course. We had a good talk, though."

"About what?"

"About everything. Even about you."

"Me?"

"Yeah. Josh was saying how much you loved your new horse

and he could tell that you were going to make something of yourself in the equestrian world."

Tears suddenly spilled from Serenity's eyes. She was too startled to feel the sadness. All she could do was bury her face between her knees. Rick looked startled too, unsure of what to do. He scooted closer and put a careful hand on her back.

"I'm sorry, Serenity," he said softly. "I didn't mean to make you cry."

Serenity shook her head and wiped her cheeks with her sleeve. "No, don't be. I'm glad you told me. He was also so kind and sweet, even if he was a little punk sometimes. That's how I remember him."

She sniffled.

"Sorry, I must look like a mess. I have the world's worst ugly cry."

"Not even close."

She gave him a grateful smile.

"What do you remember most about him?" she asked.

Rick took his hand away and settled back against the tree.

"I don't know. I wish I could say we were best pals but we were more like hang-out buddies. That time he brought me out here was the only time I was ever with him one-on-one. Usually we were just hanging out and messing around with kids from school. But one thing I do remember very clearly about him was his laugh. He was always telling jokes, and he would be the first one to laugh at them.

Usually that means your jokes are not funny, but his were, and his laugh was so infectious, it pulled you in and you were laughing with him even before you got the joke."

Serenity grinned. "You're right, that's what he did. He got it from my daddy. He does the same thing. Drives my mother nuts but a zebra can't change its stripes."

"That's for sure."

Serenity fixed her eyes on him, making him stop mid–bite.

"What?" he asked.

"You did."

"Did what?"

"Changed your stripes."

"I don't know," Rick said with a shrug. "I cleaned up my act, yeah. But I'm still me."

"I'd say becoming a Christian is more than just cleaning up your act."

"Well, you got that right. You know that verse about becoming a new creation? I really felt it when I gave my life to Christ. Still do. I'm far from perfect but I don't feel aimless like before. People think you need a dream or goal or fun job to have self–worth, and that's true in a way, but I know that my life has been bought by the blood of Jesus and that's a bigger confidence booster than anything."

He blushed when he saw the look in her eyes.

"What?"

Serenity shook her head. "Just never thought I'd hear those words coming from Rick Stevens."

"A few years ago, I'd have been right there with you. I had no need for God, or thought I had no need. But when He gets a hold of you, there's nothing you can do."

"Amen."

The bird chirped again. Rick and Serenity both looked up, then at each other, and smiled.

"It seems silly to say," Serenity said, brushing her hair back, "but I feel like Josh is watching us."

Rick stared up into the branches. "If he were here, what would he say?"

Serenity thought for a moment. "He'd probably say, 'Look at you sad sacks moping in the shade on a beautiful day like this.'"

"Yep, that sounds like Josh. I wouldn't say that he would be the first choice for a shoulder to cry on, but he always had a positive vibe. I remember we went muddin' in Jamie Foster's four–by–four right after he failed a big math test. Josh was having such a good time, you'd have thought he'd graduated with honors."

The idea of Josh hanging out of the truck window and getting spattered with mud made Serenity smile.

"You know, Rick, I didn't feel this way at first – in fact, I felt the opposite – but I'm glad you knew Josh. We all wish things had turned out different, but it's nice to know that someone else shared his happiness."

Rick reached out and touched her arm. "Me too."

Serenity felt her skin tingle. She looked into his eyes. There was so much to discover in those eyes. So much to understand...

She rose to her feet and smacked the dust off her jeans. "You reckon you're up for another ride?"

Rick stood up and pointed at the saddle on the ground. "Might be kind of difficult."

Serenity's shoulders slumped. "Shoot, I forgot. That ain't going to be cheap to fix."

"I can help you with it."

"You got a kid-sized saddle tree laying around?"

"No, I mean help you pay for it."

Serenity gave him a stern look. "Thanks, but no. I need to do things myself. And it may sound weird and selfish, but I don't want to feel like I owe you."

Rick nodded. "I can understand that. The offer still stands, but I won't step on your toes."

"Thank you." She nudged the saddle with her boot. "Well, I guess we can set the saddle on Jasmine's back and lead her real slow back to the barn so it don't fall off."

"And what about you?"

Serenity cringed.

****

Patti looked up from her magazine when Serenity came into the house.

"Just you, sweetheart?"

"Yeah. Rick had to head out."

"Did you have a good ride?"

Serenity yanked off her boots and blew the hair out of her eyes.

"Yes. At least until the cinch snapped and the saddle tree cracked."

Patti's hand flew to her mouth.

"Oh my goodness! Are you hurt?"

"I'm fine, Mama. It broke when I was getting down."

"Thank the Lord. I know you're a pro out there but I'm your mama and I still worry about you every time you go out and ride hard like that." Her eyes twinkled. "You know I was watching y'all, right?"

Serenity grinned. "Of course, Mama."

"And I noticed you two coming back on the same horse."

"That's because Jasmine's saddle was broken."

Patti frowned. "Oh, right. Well, both of y'all looked mighty content all cozied up like that."

Serenity rolled her eyes and sat down on the sofa. "Come on..."

Patti sat down and touched her knee. "Sweetheart, I'm your mother, and I'm a woman. I know how these things work. You can tell me anything. Is there a spark again?"

Serenity fell back into the soft cushions. "I don't know, Mama. What if I said yes, that I'm having feelings for him again? I mean, you saw Daddy's face when Rick said how he was testing my boundaries that night. Not to mention that he was there with Josh when he... Do we want someone like that in our family?"

"Sweetheart, what matters is what God wants for us."

"Why would God want me to be with him, after all we've been through, our history, our pain? There have to be a million other nice, sweet, drama-free guys out there."

"Perhaps. No one can make that decision but you. Listen to God, and listen to your heart."

"How come God doesn't just come out and say it? It would be so much easier if I could hear His voice as easily as I'm hearing yours."

Patti gave her daughter a gentle smile. "My sweet child, you *can* hear His words."

Serenity followed her mother's gaze to the Bible laying on the coffee table. She sighed quietly.

"You're right."

"Of course I am." Patti gave her a haughty glare, then laughed. She took Serenity's face in her hands. "The best advice I can ever give you is to read God's Word and pray with all your heart."

"I will, Mama."

Serenity nestled her head against her mother's bosom. They stayed like that for a long while.

CHAPTER FIFTEEN

GREG CAME HOME and the family had dinner together. Afterwards, they watched *Where the Red Fern Grows* on TV. Patti cried almost the entire movie. Greg cleared his throat a couple of times.

When the movie was finished, Serenity said good night to her folks and went upstairs. She showered, brushed her teeth, changed into her pajamas, and climbed into bed. The same thoughts ran through her head every night: Were the horses all right? Were they cold? Did they have enough food and water? Did they miss her?

Serenity knew they were fine, but she couldn't just turn off her worrying like a tap. She loved them and cared about them. Hopefully Hillbilly wasn't jealous that Jasmine and Crack Shot got to go for a run today. He was old enough and wise enough to know that he was still the favorite.

The phone on the nightstand buzzed and Serenity brought the screen to life. It was a message from Cassie, saying how much she missed her and wanted to catch up. She had heard about the school demo from Kelly. She had also heard that Rick was there. Serenity could see the "wink wink" in her words.

She checked her email and dropped the phone on the bed. No new messages. A few parents had "liked" her pictures on Instagram but none had contacted her directly to set up lessons. What had she done wrong? The kids loved her, right? So did the parents. And then, of course, there was Rick. They had loved him too. Especially that one blonde. Serenity's blood boiled. She let him off the hook too easily. She should have confronted him, especially since he was now a Christian. It's not a very Christian thing to take a strange woman back to his place. If that was actually where they were going... Well, where else would they be going? There weren't any parks or romantic spots in the direction he had been driving.

There was the river, though...

Serenity clenched her jaw. No. He wasn't like that anymore. He had changed his stripes.

But he'd said it himself: *"I'm still me."*

How much "me"?

Serenity looked at her phone again, scrolling through posted pictures. In the clutter of horse and fashion photos was Cal Brookfield's smiling face. Vanessa Timms was right next to him, and between them was her hand with a giant diamond ring on her finger. The caption was just one word: "YES!"

Serenity wrinkled her nose. *Well, congratulations.* Then she did something she should have done a long time ago. She unfollowed Cal's account. A weary sigh escaped her lips and she put the phone back on the nightstand. She pulled the covers up to her chin and burrowed her head into the pillow.

A strange sound reached her ears. She sat up and turned her ear toward the door.

It sounded like Mama crying.

Creeping slowly out of bed, Serenity opened the door and went to the top of the stairs. She couldn't see her parents but she could hear Mama sobbing quietly in the living room. She went down the stairs as softly as she could.

"Mama?"

Greg and Patti were on the love seat. Greg was holding a piece of paper in his hand.

"Mama?" Serenity repeated. "What is it?"

Patti wiped her eyes. "Oh honey, I'm sorry I woke you up."

"It's fine, Mama. Tell me what's wrong."

Greg gestured to the paper. "The bank's threatening to foreclose on us."

Patti began weeping again. Serenity took a seat and embraced her mother's trembling shoulders.

"It'll be okay, Mama."

Greg looked confused. Patti wiped her eyes and touched his

hand. "I told her. She needed to know."

Greg didn't look happy but he nodded. Patti turned to Serenity and forced a smile.

"You're right, sweetheart. It isn't a surprise, but just knowing that it's here is...is just..."

Fresh sobs broke though and she rested her head on Serenity's shoulder.

Greg crumpled the paper and threw it across the room. "This house and land have been in my family for three generations. It's my fault we're in this mess. If I had learned to be a halfway decent rancher or even work with horses like you, Serenity, I might have been able to make something of this place. Instead, I got this useless store and fifty acres I ain't using for squat."

"So what now?" Serenity asked.

"We sell to the Fairbaughs and work out a deal where we can stay on the land."

It was painful to hear the words. Serenity looked away. Patti touched her hand.

"Sweetheart, you know this also means that we won't have a place for the horses anymore."

Serenity choked back her own tears. "I know, Mama."

She looked at her parents with determination in her eyes.

"I'll call Aunt Lillian and see if she'll have me up at her place. I'm thinking this is God's way of pushing me out of the nest."

"Oh, sweetheart..." Patti gave her a tearful hug, and Greg followed. Despite the sadness and uncertainty, it was so nice just sitting in their embrace. Serenity blinked away her tears and sat up.

"You told me to pray, Mama. I think we should pray now."

"I agree," Greg said.

They all closed their eyes.

"Dear Lord," Serenity prayed, "please guide us through this challenge. Don't let us be anxious for anything, but let us rest in Your strength and wisdom, especially when we're scared. Thank You that You love us and we know You'll take care of us no matter what. In Jesus' name, amen."

"Amen."

"Amen."

Greg let out a deep breath and threaded his fingers together.

"I'm so sorry," he said, his voice small and broken. "I feel like I've failed you."

Patti and Serenity gave him warm hugs. "That's impossible," Patti said. "You're the best man I know and that's what matters."

"And we're not on the streets, Daddy," Serenity added. "We still have a home, you still have a job. We'll be all right."

Greg smiled sadly. "Thank you."

Serenity rose to her feet. "I should get back to bed."

"Okay." Patti reached out and took her hand. "We're so sorry about all this, sweetheart. No child should have to go through something like this."

"There are lots of things we *shouldn't* go through, Mama, but we do. It's part of trusting that God knows better than we do, right?"

Patti's eyes sparkled. "Right."

Serenity gave her parents kisses on the cheek. "Good night, y'all. I love you."

"We love you too, sweetheart."

Serenity went back upstairs and crawled into bed. She pressed her face against her pillow and let the tears flow.

*****

"Miss Serenity? Miss Serenity?"

The grass was so beautiful in November. Serenity didn't know why she hadn't noticed it before.

"Miss Serenity!"

She snapped her head back. "Yes, Alice?"

"Um, I think you should hold the line."

Serenity looked down. The lead line was dragging on the ground. Hillbilly had been following her around simply because he wanted to.

"Sorry," she stammered as she grabbed the line. The little girl's face relaxed when she saw that her teacher had a hold of the horse she was riding.

Serenity led Alice and Hillbilly around the arena a few times. She had thought about trying a trot or even putting the bridle on Hillbilly and letting Alice take the reins, but even though the little girl might be ready for it, Serenity just didn't feel like putting in the effort today. Luckily, Alice didn't seem to notice, and when her mother came to pick her up, she was all smiles. Her mother thanked Serenity and left with Alice. The way things were going lately, Serenity was half-expecting her to cancel her classes too.

It didn't really matter, anyway. She was going to have to close up shop here soon. She still hadn't called Aunt Lillian, even though it had been three days since her parents broke the news to her. There was just something so definite, so *final,* about making a call like that. Yet she knew the longer she waited, the more she jeopardized her future and the future of her family. She didn't know if Daddy had talked to the Fairbaughs yet about buying the land. It had to happen, of course, but part of her wished he wouldn't. There had to be another way, there had to be some solution…

Hillbilly nudged her arm and she pressed her cheek against his. He could always tell when something was troubling her. He was such a sweet horse. They all were. It broke Serenity's heart afresh when she thought of them leaving here, never galloping over these gentle hills again, never grazing beneath the towering oak trees that had endured for generations.

She had to remind herself that they weren't going to prison or being put down or anything. Aunt Lillian's place up in Nebraska was amazing. A bit flat, but stretching from horizon to horizon, far bigger than her family's fifty acres. And she had a proper school up there, with over a dozen horses at least. Hillbilly, Jasmine, and Crack Shot would be happy in a place like that.

...assuming she would be able to bring them.

A knot tightened in Serenity's stomach. What if she wasn't able to bring all of the horses up there? Aunt Lillian wouldn't make her leave one, or two, or *all* of them behind. Would she?

Serenity was dreading the phone call now more than ever. It was awful, hovering in limbo among all of the "what ifs." She wished she could turn off the runaway anxiety train in her mind but there was no stopping those wheels on the track. She wondered if this was the way life was always going to be, hopping from one freak-out to the next.

She sighed and patted Hillbilly's shoulder.

"You're lucky you're a horse."

Hillbilly nudged her hand. Serenity looked up at the deep blue sky and inhaled the fresh autumn air. This wasn't the end of the world. This wasn't what she or her family had planned, but maybe it was God's plan. And He always knows best.

After putting Hillbilly away and feeding and grooming the horses and mucking the stalls, Serenity went outside and leaned against a tree. She thought of Rick. She didn't know why, but he just popped into her head. He had been doing that a lot lately after their pleasant ride. The ride that resulted in a broken saddle. Serenity winced when she remembered. Fortunately the one saddle she had left wasn't too big but it wasn't ideal for children riders. Guess it didn't matter now, anyway. They must have saddles a-plenty up at Aunt Lillian's.

Serenity kicked a rock and marched up the hill toward the house. Instead of going inside, she got in her truck and started the engine. Mama wasn't home so it wasn't like she was skipping out on lunch. But lunch was what she needed right now. A big bowl of the spiciest chili in town, and there was only one place to get it: the same diner where she had seen Rick and that blonde woman.

Well, she was just going to have to suppress that irritating memory. As she drove down the driveway to the road, she could already taste Harry's red bean-and-venison chili.

Fifteen minutes later, she pulled into the parking lot. When she stepped out of the truck, she glanced to her left. Her heart froze.

There was a red, late-model Chevy pickup truck three spaces down.

Rick was here *again*.

Serenity arched her neck to look into the diner's windows but she didn't see him. She wasn't at a very good angle though, and she missed all of the windows toward the back.

She leaned against her truck and considered her options. She could go in there and see him, pretend it was a happy coincidence, which it was, and go over and join him. Or she could go in there and see him, hope he didn't see her, and then when he walked past as she was eating her lunch, she could act surprised to see him. Which was the better choice? She wasn't really sure.

Then there was the third option: that she goes in there and doesn't see him, but he sees her. Would he invite her over to his table or would he come join her? Surely he wouldn't just smile and nod and keep eating his lunch, right?

Serenity's hands were starting to feel sweaty despite the cool temperature outside. Her stomach growled impatiently. She looked at the diner and tried to quell the storm buffeting her mind.

Doggone it, girl! Go in there and get some food!

Rick or no Rick, she was going in there and getting that spicy chili. She glanced in her truck's side mirror to make sure she wasn't a complete mess and walked up to the door. When she stepped inside, she quickly scanned the diner. Her eyes locked on a booth toward the back.

She hadn't considered the fourth option.

Rick was here, all right. And he wasn't alone. He and the blonde woman were leaning over their food, talking very seriously.

The heat rose in Serenity's cheeks. A waitress walked up to her and asked her where she'd like to sit but she brushed on by. She marched toward Rick and that blonde woman snuggled up together in that booth, looking as happy as two birds in a nest. She wasn't sure what she would do when she got over there but she knew it wasn't going to be pretty.

Rick looked up when she approached. His face flushed red and his eyes grew wide.

"Serenity!" He looked at the blonde woman and smiled awkwardly.

Serenity's eyes were as cold as ice. "Hi, Rick," she stated like she was reading the news. "How are you?"

Before he could answer, she turned to the blonde and stuck out her hand. "Serenity MacAlister."

The blonde woman shook her hand and gave her a sweet smile. "Kathy Brown."

Serenity returned the smile, her face tight as a drum. "I remember you from my demo at the elementary school."

"Yes," Kathy said, shooting a quick glance toward Rick. "I enjoyed it very much."

"So did the kids. Tell me, whose mother are you?"

"Serenity."

"Yes, Rick?"

Rick reached out and took a chair from a neighboring table. "Sit down."

"Oh, no thanks. I don't want to interrupt your lunch. I just wanted to come over and say hi. And I'm glad you liked the demo,

Mrs. Brown, though it seems that Rick was more of the star of the show."

"Serenity," Rick repeated.

She ignored him. "In fact, I'm surprised more mothers haven't asked him for private lessons, though maybe he'll consider it since he seems to have a knack for sales."

"Serenity!"

She looked at him with daggers in her eyes. His face was beet red. Kathy was trying to hide her smile.

"Sit...down," he said through clenched teeth.

Serenity glared at him for another moment, then complied. Rick exhaled and looked at Kathy.

"Should we just tell her?"

Serenity looked at the two of them. "Tell me *what?*"

Kathy nodded and gave Serenity a dazzling smile.

"Miss MacAlister – "

"Serenity, please." How could a mom be this gorgeous? It was infuriating.

"Serenity. I'm not a mother of any of the kids at Jonesburg Elementary School."

Rick coughed. Serenity blinked.

"Then why were you at the demo?" she asked.

Kathy and Rick locked eyes for a moment. A dozen possible answers sprouted in Serenity's imagination, none of them good.

"I was there," Kathy explained, "because Rick asked me to come see your horsemanship."

Serenity gave Rick a confused look. "Why? What's going on? Who are you?"

Kathy opened her designer handbag and pulled out a business card. "I am a real estate agent. I represent Horton Ranches."

Serenity looked at the card with wide eyes. "Horton Ranches? The...the Western experience thing for them rich city folks?"

"Mm–hmm. We have eleven locations across the Midwest and Southwest. And we're looking to make it twelve."

Serenity turned to Rick. "I don't understand."

"She wants to buy my uncle's land and turn it into a Horton Ranch," he said.

Serenity gasped. She turned to Kathy with hands raised in supplication. "Oh my gosh! I am so sorry! I thought you two were..."

It sounded too ridiculous to even say out loud. Kathy let her off the hook with a smile.

"No problem at all. We've had our eye on opening a ranch in this county for a while, and when we heard that Rick's property was available, I came up from Dallas to check it out. And I was very impressed. The place needs some work but we already have clients who have asked for a ranch in this general location."

Serenity grabbed Rick's hands. "That's great!"

Then she frowned. "So why did you want to see my

horsemanship?"

Kathy gave Rick another knowing grin. "Rick said that if you wanted, you could be part of the deal."

"What do you mean?"

"You would work for the ranch," Rick said. "Trainer, wrangler, trail guide, showing those city boys how it's done. Plus, the ranch would bring their own horses in. I told Kathy that you have room in your barn, and they could board their horses there when they're not being used or if they're in need of special attention."

"And Horton Ranches pays very well," Kathy added.

Serenity stared at the table. She felt like she couldn't breathe. Rick looked at her with concern.

"Serenity? Are you all right?"

She looked up at him with shimmering eyes.

"Tell me you're serious. Tell me you're not just pulling my leg."

Rick looked baffled. "Of course not! I've been working on this even before I came to town. I didn't want to tell you at first in case things didn't work out and I got your hopes up for nothing. But we signed the paperwork yesterday and it's a done deal. We were just going over the time frame today."

"Once we get the construction permits," Kathy said, "we can get the property looking like a Horton Ranch in a matter of months and be ready by next summer. During that time, we'll put you through orientation and training, all paid of course. That is, assuming you'll say yes."

Yes! Yes!

Serenity wiped her eyes and smiled to cover her embarrassment. "This all sounds really great, and I'd love for the chance to work with y'all. It's just a little overwhelming to hear all this when I was only thinking about getting some chili today."

"I hear that," Rick said with a grin. He signaled the waitress and pointed to Serenity.

"What'll ya have, sweetie?" the waitress asked, her notepad at the ready.

"On me," Kathy said with a wink.

Serenity could only laugh as a single tear ran down her cheek.

CHAPTER SIXTEEN

HER PARENTS WERE equally stunned when she shared the news with them that night. Patti leaped off the love seat and showered her daughter with kisses. Greg just sat in his chair, looking like he'd been hit with a cannonball. Fortunately he hadn't yet called the Fairbaughs to accept their offer on the land. He said he'd have to look at the financials to see what the numbers would look like for boarding Horton horses, and he also declared that he wasn't going to have his daughter support her own parents. That's when Serenity told him that she had asked Kathy about Mr. Mac's Hunting and Fishing Supplies being the exclusive supplier of hunting and tackle equipment for this Horton Ranch location. Kathy had said that if Greg could give them a fair shake and had the right items in stock, then she didn't see why not. Horton Ranches always supported local businesses whenever they could because it helped build goodwill with the community. That turned Greg's shellshocked expression into delight. He grabbed Serenity and gave her a great big hug that took her breath away.

Serenity hardly slept that night, she was so excited. The next morning, she couldn't wait to go down to the barn and tell the horses the good news. But first, she knelt down by her bed and folded her hands.

"Lord," she prayed, "I'm sorry that I only come to you when I need something. But I know You love to take care of Your children, and I thank You for the wonderful news yesterday. I feel so silly for not trusting You to take care of us, and even when things seem helpless, Your miracles are just a moment away. Thank You so much for Your blessings. Thank You for my family, for my horses, for our home. And thank You for opening this door for us. Please let everything work out all right and give me the strength to face this new challenge. Thank You for everything that You do for us, Lord. I love You. In Jesus' name, Amen."

She rose from her knees and grabbed her hat. Today was a beautiful day for a ride.

****

Rick gave the saw one final thrust and the section of the two-by-four fell away. He wiped his brow, grimacing as flecks of sawdust from his gloves dug into his skin. He pulled them off and slapped them against his jeans, wiping his brow again with his sweaty forearm.

He squinted up at the noonday sun and went over to the cooler to grab a bottle of water. It was unseasonably warm for mid–November. There had even been chatter on the radio about the possibility of some serious thunderstorms around Thanksgiving. It wouldn't be unprecedented but it would definitely be unusual.

After taking several gulps, he went back over to the pile of lumber. He picked up another two–by–four and laid it across the sawhorses, measured twice and then drew a line with a carpenter's pencil. He had just made his first cut when he saw the cloud of dust coming up the driveway.

Serenity parked next to his truck and stepped out.

"Howdy," she said, flicking the brim of her hat.

"Howdy," he replied. He didn't try to hide his smile.

Serenity smiled back and then turned around to get something from the back seat of the truck.

"Brought you some lunch," she said as she walked over with a basket.

Rick set the saw down and took the basket from her. A sandwich, fruit, and what looked like a very delectable slice of cake.

"How'd you know I'd be here?" he asked.

Serenity shrugged. "Call it a hunch. Though I'm not sure why you're working on this place when Mrs. Brown said that she was going to have the construction permits in two shakes."

Rick looked up at the house. "I don't know... I guess I just need something to do. Plus I want to put as much of myself into this property before it belongs to a multi-state corporation. The way me and Kathy worked it out is that this house will be the main office along with a bed-and-breakfast. City folks like that sort of thing. They don't want to come stay on a compound. From what I hear, Horton Ranches goes for as authentic as possible, even though they are still a multi-state corporation. I don't think Kathy's just blowing smoke up my rear. I really think it will be a place that me, you, and my uncle would be proud of."

Serenity nodded, impressed. Rick hefted the basket in his hands.

"I'm starving, actually. Care to join me?"

"I already ate."

"Mind if I do?"

"That's why I brought it over here."

They went over to the porch steps and sat down. Serenity noticed that most of the boards had been replaced. She studied the house and saw that the shutters were new, the windows had been fixed, there was a new doorknob on the front door, and several new pieces of siding had been installed.

"Looking good," she declared. "Are you getting paid for this?"

Rick took a bite of the ham-and-cheese sandwich and shook his head. "Nope. Told Kathy what I was doing and she was like, 'Go for it.' The weather is perfect for this kind of manual labor. I figure

I'll work until the first cold snap."

Serenity brushed her hair back. "And then what?"

"What?"

"When you're done, what next?"

Rick swallowed hard. He looked directly into her eyes.

"Not sure. Just kind of taking it one day at a time, asking God for direction."

"Has He said anything yet?"

"Not yet." He took another bite. "You?"

Serenity turned aside to hide the redness in her cheeks. "Well, I think I'm going to take Kathy up on her offer. Our family's really struggling to keep our place, and it's pretty much my fault since our land is so big and the only reason we have it is for sentimental value from Daddy's family and for the horses to run around. We were actually on the verge of selling to the neighbors when you and Kathy swooped in. That's kind of why I was so emotional at the diner the other day."

"You don't need to explain. And I'm sorry for keeping it from you. I know I've let you down in many ways before and I didn't want to take the chance of doing it again, so I waited until I was sure to tell you."

"Thanks."

Serenity watched a small bug crawl across the step at her feet. "Rick?"

"Mmm?"

"I've asked you this before but you never really gave me a straight answer. Did you come back to Jonesburg for me?"

Rick chewed slowly, swallowed slowly, then took a slow drink of water. He brushed the crumbs off his hands and looked out across the grass.

"Yes."

Serenity's heart jumped. She kept her face blank.

"Why?"

"Hard to say, I guess." Rick threaded his fingers together and took a deep breath. "I wanted to make things right with you and your family, as much as I could. Especially you. And I wanted to make this deal happen, but even if it didn't, I wanted to be around you. It was selfish of me to just waltz into your life again, but I felt like I was being pulled back here, like gravity. I wanted to be..."

She looked up at him, eyes shaded from the sun.

"What?"

"I wanted you to see who I was now."

"Why did you want me to see who you are now?"

"Because I didn't just want to be a bad memory for you. Someone you thought of when you're feeling down, someone that you're glad is no longer in your life. I care about you, Serenity. I always have. I thought about you all the time when I was deployed. And when I got saved, all I could think about was coming back here and seeing you again."

Serenity kept her eyes fixed on him. Her heart was pounding and she folded her hands together to stop them from trembling.

"Thank you for telling me, Rick," she said, using all of her effort to keep her voice steady. "You've succeeded very well in replacing my bad memory of you with a good one."

He rose to his feet. "Is that all I'll be? A good memory?"

Serenity also stood up. "I..."

The breeze stirred her hair, blowing against her back. Pushing her toward him. She gripped the wooden railing.

"I can't say yet, Rick. I wish I could."

Rick nodded slowly. Serenity studied his face. She couldn't tell if he was disappointed or just agreeing with her.

A quiet moment passed between them.

Say something.

Serenity opened her mouth, then closed it and looked at her boots.

"I, uh, I got to be heading back. Horses need feeding."

Rick nudged the basket with his boot. "Don't we all."

Serenity grinned. "Well, don't work too hard out here. And make sure you apply sunscreen. Just because it's November don't mean the sun won't burn you."

"Yes, ma'am."

Serenity gave him a shrewd look and walked over to her truck.

When she opened the door, Rick held up the basket.

"You forgot this," he said.

"Bring it over next time."

Rick frowned. "Next time?"

"Mama said you're invited to Thanksgiving dinner next week."

She watched a slow smile spread across his face.

Serenity tipped her hat and put the truck in reverse. When she shifted into drive and drove down the driveway, she saw him standing on the porch, holding the food basket.

Her heart was still racing.

God, what in the heck am I doing?

****

"Grab that oven mitt, sweetie."

Serenity picked it up off the counter and handed it to Patti, who opened the bottom oven and pulled out the rack to inspect the sweet potato casserole.

"About fifteen more minutes," she declared, sliding the dish back inside and closing up the oven. Serenity nodded her approval, even though she knew her opinion didn't matter when it came to cooking the sweet potato casserole.

She looked around the kitchen, marveling at how such elegant and delicious dishes could come from such a mess. And this was after the turkey had been stuffed and shoved into the top oven. She and Mama had been working hard all day, putting together what was shaping up to be quite a Thanksgiving feast.

Daddy was in the living room, watching football. He had made a half-hearted effort to help, knowing what the answer was before he asked the question. Mama informed him that the barbecue out back was his territory, and the kitchen was hers. He gladly agreed and turned his attention back to the game.

Serenity looked at the clock on the wall. 4:15. Rick was supposed to come over around 5:30, a little before sunset. She looked out the window and furrowed her brow. With those heavy, dark clouds in the sky, there wasn't going to be any sunset tonight. The rain hadn't started falling yet but there was a frightful wind blowing hard against the house. It felt more like Halloween than Thanksgiving. Last year was warm and sunny, and the year before that, they had an early frost but it made everything look magical. This kind of stormy weather belonged in August, not November.

She looked at Patti, her worry evident on her face. Patti spoke before she could.

"Don't fret none, sweetie. The weatherman said there won't be no twisters or nothing, just some wind and rain. Not particularly ideal weather but we should be all the more thankful that we have a warm, dry house to eat our food in. It's easy to forget the blessings we have."

"That's true."

Serenity looked outside again, unable to calm the storm in her own mind.

"Still, I'll be praying the whole time that this blows over. The horses won't be used to it this late in the year, and I don't want them to get spooked in case it starts to lightning."

Patti gave her a reassuring smile. "I'll pray too. In the meantime, I'll get to work on these dishes and you can set out the china." She took a deep breath and looked off to the side for a moment. "Did we do the right thing, inviting Rick over?"

"What do you mean?" Serenity asked as she went to the cupboard where the china was kept.

Patti turned on the faucet and began scrubbing a mixing bowl. "I don't wonder if inviting that half-starved boy over here to eat with us is the right thing, as in the Christian thing to do. I just wonder if we...I mean, I...might be pushing all of us too hard for reconciliation. The heart can be so strong yet so fragile sometimes. I want things to be right between all of us; I just hope the glue is dry before we do any moving."

Serenity put her hands on her hips. "That's mighty poetic, Mama."

Patti blushed. "Oh, get on now. But I'm serious, though. Is this okay for us?"

Serenity set down the stack of plates and walked over to her. "Yes, Mama," she said, giving her a hug. "I wouldn't have agreed if I didn't feel the same way about Rick. I can't speak for Daddy but I'm sure he does too. Things have come a long way since he showed up, and he deserves not only our forgiveness, but also our thanks."

"You're right," Patti said quietly.

"Git 'em!"

Serenity and Patti flinched as Greg's voice shook the house. The two women shared a laugh and Serenity started setting the table. As she placed the soup spoons to the right of the teaspoons and folded the napkins into a simple flower shape, she remembered her mother's advice and prayed.

****

After the table was set and the food was nearly ready, Serenity went upstairs to her bedroom to change. She passed by Josh's room and paused. The door opened with a creak and she peeked her head in. It was spotless, as usual. Serenity glanced around the room, at the posters on the wall, at the books and trophies and pictures on the shelves. She could picture him sitting at the desk, his back to her, headphones on, head bobbing to music as he did his homework. He would feel her watching him and turn around and smile, maybe throw a wad of paper at her. She would snatch his candy from his dresser and rush down the hall, stuffing it in her mouth before he could chase after her and catch her. He would tickle her until she spat out colorful candy pieces and Mama would come upstairs to break up the gentle fight.

Serenity let the flood of memories and emotions wash over her for a few moments. She whispered, "Miss you, bro," and closed the door.

The clothes she was wearing smelled like the kitchen and she tossed them in the hamper. She put on a fresh pair of jeans and a green shirt with dark gray buttons. Satisfied with how she looked below the neck, she turned her attention to her face. She brushed her hair and got out her curling iron, adding some bouncy ringlets

Makeup was next. She decided on some light mascara and just a little blush on her cheeks. She wanted to look her prettiest but she didn't want it to look obvious that she wanted to look her prettiest. It took a couple of tries to get her eyelashes right, and after a moment of consideration, she worked on her eyebrows a little. Some lip gloss completed the ensemble and she studied her face in the mirror. Everyone always told her how pretty she was and she knew it was true, but it was hard not to see all of the minute imperfections that she wished she could just Photoshop away.

She sighed, then smiled. Life didn't work like that, but it was all right. Like Daddy said, we should be thankful for what we have and what we don't. There was just one thing missing.

A quick search on top of her dresser turned up the sky blue ribbon for her hair. She tied it in a bow behind her head and turned to look at it in the mirror. It was such a small, simple thing, but it made everything look better. She hoped Rick noticed.

Right at that moment, headlights swept across the front yard. Serenity's heart jumped.

It's Thanksgiving with your family, not a candlelight dinner in Paris.

She took a deep breath and looked herself over in the mirror one last time. She didn't know why she was so nervous.

Actually, she knew exactly why.

CHAPTER SEVENTEEN

GREG OPENED THE DOOR and Rick stepped inside.

"Howdy, Mr. MacAlister."

Greg shook his hand. "Glad you could make it."

"Welcome, Rick," Patti said, stepping up to give him a kiss on the cheek.

Rick smiled and handed her a platter covered with tin foil. "I ain't really got a kitchen so I couldn't whip up anything to bring y'all, but I picked up an apple pie from Suzy's. I hope that isn't intruding on any pies you might have already made."

Patti took the pie with a smile. "We have a pumpkin pie but this will make a nice second option."

Rick nodded his thanks. Beets curled around his feet and purred when Rick scratched behind his ears. "Where's Serenity?"

The top step creaked, and everyone turned and looked up.

Serenity came down the stairs with a beaming smile. She saw Rick's eyes grow wide and her heart fluttered again.

"Well, look at you," Greg said, holding out his hand to her as she reached the floor. "Pretty as a summer's day."

Serenity looked at Rick. He was staring at her like an open–mouthed fool.

"Hi, Rick," she said, brushing her hair back behind her hear.

Rick swallowed. "Hi, Serenity. I like the ribbon in your hair."

"Thanks." She tried to hold his gaze but her eyes fell away.

Patti smiled at the two of them for a moment, then ushered everyone into the kitchen. "Come on now, enough gawking. Time to make our bellies happy."

Greg offered his arm and Serenity let him lead her into the dining room. She didn't notice him wink at Rick behind her.

Serenity and Rick sat down and awkwardly smiled at each other as Patti and Greg brought out the dishes. Sweet potato casserole, rolls, cranberry sauce, fried okra, and of course, the turkey. Every year, Patti fretted that it was too dry, and every year, it was scrumptious. Greg had offered to deep fry it but Patti refused, saying that she wanted to preserve her mother's tradition, and Greg was only too happy to oblige. After the sweet tea was poured, Greg and Patti sat down and everyone joined hands.

"Dear Lord," Greg prayed, "thank You for the blessings You have given us this year, and every year. Thank You that we can share our table with Your child Rick. Thank You for giving us Your grace and salvation, and thank You for the beautiful hands that have prepared this food. In Your Son's blessed name, Amen."

"Amen," everyone agreed.

Lightning flashed and thunder cracked, shaking the plates and silverware. Serenity looked fearfully at her father, who gave her hand a reassuring squeeze.

"My, my," Patti said, trying to hide her worry with a smile, "that was quite an 'amen'."

"Can't remember the last time we had a Thanksgiving storm," Greg said as he rose to carve the turkey. "Reminds us that we should all be thankful for a dry roof over our heads. It's one of the easiest things to forget about."

"Yes, sir," Rick said, taking a sip of sweet tea. He set down his glass and cleared his throat. "I just want to thank all y'all for having me over here tonight. Y'all have really been such a blessing to me since I got back, more than I ever expected. I can truly see God's love in y'all's hearts, and from the bottom of mine, I thank y'all."

Patti's eyes shimmered as she raised her glass. "And thank you, Rick, for being a blessing in our life. God really does work in mysterious ways."

Serenity raised her glass as well. "Amen."

They clinked glasses. Serenity's eyes met Rick's as she sipped her sweet tea.

"All right," Greg announced, "get your bird."

Serenity held out her plate for Daddy to place a slab of meat.

He knew she loved the white meat and Mama liked the dark. He didn't ask Rick which he preferred, giving him dark meat. Rick seemed happy with the choice, smothering the meat in gravy before taking a large bite.

"Do you miss your family?" Patti asked.

"I suppose," Rick said, his mouth still full. "I miss the good ol' days with them, but not the more recent ones. There weren't a lot of happy days in my family's home before I went off to the basic. I suppose that's one reason why I was so glad to be away."

Patti touched his arm. "I'm sorry. I didn't mean to bring up bad memories."

Rick shook his head. "Don't be. I've made my peace with the situation, and I've been praying for all of them since I got saved, especially my dad. I can feel God working in my heart with this. I feel like I should be angry but I'm not. I suppose that's the 'peace that passes all understanding'."

"Amen," Greg said, taking a bite of turkey. "That's one thing that makes the pain and sorrows of life bearable, seeing God work His miracles in the midst of those trials. Ain't that right, honey?"

"Sure is," Patti said. She looked at Serenity with gentle eyes. "It's in our fear and despair that God shows Himself most vividly."

Serenity blushed, not knowing why. She dabbed her mouth with a napkin as an excuse to turn her face away.

Thunder boomed outside and rain spattered the kitchen

window. Serenity's stomach clenched.

"You think the horses are all right?" she asked.

"I'm sure they're fine," Patti said, though her expression betrayed her uncertainty.

Serenity took a bite of sweet potato casserole, trying to ignore the sound of raindrops pounding against the side of the house. Hillbilly was an old pro but Jasmine and Crack Shot were quite a bit younger. They were probably wild-eyed with fear right now...

"Serenity."

She turned to her father and saw the calmness in his eyes.

"They'll be fine," he said. "We can go out and check on them after we eat."

"Okay," Serenity agreed, trying to undo the knot in her stomach. She took a tepid bite of turkey, squeezing her eyes shut when lightning flashed again.

A crack of thunder shook the whole house. Serenity pushed herself away from the table and jumped to her feet.

"I'm sorry," she cried, "but I have to go out and make sure they're okay!"

"Serenity!" Patti exclaimed.

Rick leaped up as well. "I'll go out with her."

Serenity was already at the door, pulling on her coat. "I'll be fine," she said.

"I'm coming with you."

She saw the determination in his face, and she saw the anxiety in her parents' eyes.

"We'll be fine," she said as she opened the door. She was immediately spattered with raindrops and Rick lunged forward to grab the door.

"I'll go!" Greg bellowed. "You kids stay here."

"They're my horses, Daddy," Serenity said firmly. She looked at Rick, then rushed out into the storm.

Rick glanced at Patti and Greg.

"Be careful!" Patti gasped.

Rick nodded and followed after Serenity.

The wind howled in her ears and the raindrops pelted her skin like bee stings, but Serenity thought only about her horses as she leaned forward against the wind. Rick grabbed her arm and she felt a swell of comfort that he was by her side. He wrapped his arm around her and together they trudged forward, utterly soaked after just a few seconds.

When they drew near to the barn, Serenity could hear the horses crying out inside. She gasped and rushed forward, gripping the door and pulling it open. She fell into the welcoming dryness inside and Rick jumped in after her.

The three horses stamped and stirred in their stalls, though Jasmine and Crack Shot appeared especially agitated. They whinnied and blustered when they saw the humans. Serenity reached out and stroked Jasmine's nose and she immediately calmed down. Rick also comforted Hillbilly, then went over to Crack Shot's stall.

"Easy, boy," he said, extending his hand.

Crack Shot cried out and reared back on his hind legs. Serenity saw the panic in his eyes and she left Jasmine to go over to him.

"Shh, shh..."

It hurt her heart to see him so frightened. The horse was in a full-fledged panic, pacing around his tiny stall and stamping his hooves. Serenity looked at Rick with worry.

"He's terrified," she lamented. Rick squeezed her hand.

Lightning blazed, followed by a violent crash of thunder. Crack Shot wailed again, kicking the walls of the stall.

Serenity couldn't take it anymore. She unlocked the door to the stall and stepped inside to comfort him.

A blinding flash of lightning seared the sky and Crack Shot reared back, his eyes wide with terror. Before Serenity could react, the horse bolted out of the stall, knocking Rick off his feet.

"Crack Shot!" Serenity screamed, watching the horse rush out of the barn and disappear into the storm.

She helped Rick to his feet.

"Are you all right?"

Rick nodded, looking shaken.

Serenity stared out into the darkness.

"We have to get him back!" she cried.

Rick took her hand. "Where's the saddle?"

A couple of minutes later, they rode Hillbilly out into the rain, Rick in front with Serenity behind him, holding tight to his shirt. Rain stabbed their eyes as they searched the darkness.

"Crack Shot!" Serenity called out into the storm. "Where are you?"

"We'll find him," Rick said, urging Hillbilly forward. The horse blustered but he obeyed, lowered his head and pushing against the wind and rain.

Serenity squinted against the rain, her heart breaking with every passing second.

"Rick, where is he?"

"We'll find him!" Rick called back to her.

She clung to him as he nudged Hillbilly ahead. They had no light to see around them; the only illumination came from flashes of lightning, and Serenity knew that each lightning bolt sent fear and terror through the heart of her already terrified horse. Even Hillbilly was upset but he had enough presence of mind to maintain control of his stride.

Rick and Serenity called out into the darkness as the wind and rain pushed against them. Lightning flashed and thunder crashed, illuminating the grassy hills for fractions of a second, but they couldn't see Crack Shot in those fleeting glimpses.

Serenity's tears mingled with the rain flowing down her face.

Please God...Please...

"Crack Shot!" Rick called out. "Here, boy!"

Thunder boomed. There was another sound. A frightened whinny.

Rick and Serenity squinted as they peered into the rain and darkness.

Lightning flashed. In the ghastly glow, they could make out the grove of trees at the southeast corner of the property.

Just below the trees was the shape of a horse.

Serenity gasped. "Rick! There!"

Rick wiped the water from his eyes and flicked the reins. "Hyah!"

Hillbilly felt his way through the darkness, sensing the urgency of the situation. Serenity tightened her grip on Rick's shirt as they went down into a shallow valley and started climbing the hill.

Another flash of lightning. Crack Shot was half a dozen yards away. Rick leaped off the horse and ran through the rain, clutching the halter in his fist. Serenity jumped forward onto the saddle and took the reins.

"Rick!" she cried out.

Thunder crashed.

"Rick!"

Rain pounded her eyes and ears. She whipped her head back and forth, searching the darkness around her.

"Rick! Where are you?"

A bright blue bolt of lightning crawled across the sky. In the surreal glow, she saw Rick's silhouette beneath the trees. He had slipped the halter over Crack Shot's head and was holding tight onto the lead line.

Serenity's heart leaped. She snapped the reins and Hillbilly ran toward the grove of trees. Once she was under the cover of branches, she dismounted and wrapped the reins around a low–hanging branch.

Rick and Crack Shot were next to a nearby tree. Serenity ran over to them, tears streaming down her cheeks as she hugged her horse's neck. Rick tied the lead line to a branch and bent down to catch his breath.

"He's fine," he panted.

Serenity turned around and jumped forward, wrapping her arms around Rick's neck and pressing a kiss to his mouth. The shock took Rick's breath away for a moment, then he embraced her tightly and kissed her back as rain drops fell from the leaves above them.

Lightning flashed. Thunder boomed. Serenity pulled her lips away from his. Then she gasped and shrank back.

Rick held out his hands in surprise. "What's wrong?"

Serenity's heart was pounding. She staggered back, and her hand touched her lips in disbelief.

"Serenity..." Rick took a step toward her.

"No!" she cried out, turning away.

She felt his strong hands grip her shoulders. Tears burst from her eyes as she turned around. She could barely see him in the darkness but she could feel his warmth.

"Serenity," he said, his voice quivering, "I love you. I always have. I didn't know how to show you before, and I don't even know how to show you now, but I love you, deep down in my heart."

"Rick," she sobbed, "I...I don't know..."

"Don't know what?"

She shrugged out of his grasp and fell back against a tree.

"I don't know!" she wailed. "I don't know what I feel!"

"Why not?"

"Because!"

"Because what?"

"Because I can't forgive myself!"

She sank to the ground, weeping into her hands. The horses whinnied and stamped as thunder cracked, though it was more distant this time.

Rick knelt down in front of her. He touched her shoulder.

"Serenity..."

She looked up at him with tears streaming down her cheeks. "I can't forgive myself, Rick! Every time I look at myself, every time I look at you, I see the people that killed Josh! How can we live with that?"

Rick embraced her and held her close. She wept against his chest and she felt his body tremble with hers.

"I don't know," he said softly, his own voice choked with tears. "I see the same thing too when I look at myself. Every day, I pray for the strength to accept God's forgiveness."

Serenity wiped her eyes and looked up at him. "What if I can't?"

Even in the darkness, she could see the tenderness in his eyes. "I'll pray for both of us."

She reached up to touch his face. Her lips parted. "I love you, Rick Stevens."

He pulled her close and they kissed again, soft and deep. Soothing warmth spread across Serenity's skin as she let her fear and worries slip away, feeling an indescribable peace as she lay in Rick's strong arms, pressing her lips to his. She loved him. With all of her heart, she loved him.

The world seemed to hold its breath as they kissed and held each other close. The storm fell quiet and the horses didn't seem as agitated. In her mind, Serenity knew how foolish this was. She was outside in a rain storm, sitting in the mud in the arms of a man who had broken her heart and was forever connected to her family's tragedy. But the love and joy swelling in her heart overwhelmed her mind's objections, which were pretty wimpy anyway. She knew this was right, even though it didn't make sense.

And she knew that *he* was right. They were going to have to learn to forgive themselves, just as God had forgiven them.

For the first time in a long time, she realized that the serenity she had been named for was within her reach.

She looked into his soft, gentle eyes and touched his handsome face.

"What are we doing?" she whispered.

Rick shook his head and smiled. "I don't know. I just know what I feel. I want to make you the happiest woman alive, Serenity MacAlister."

She smiled back and stroked his chin. "You're off to a pretty good start."

He kissed her once more, and she could feel herself melting in his arms. If she could, she would have frozen that moment for all eternity.

Thunder rumbled in the distance and Crack Shot stamped nervously. Serenity wiped the rain from her eyes and looked at the horses.

"We need to get them back," she said, reluctantly pulling herself out of Rick's embrace and standing up. Rick stood up with her. They looked over one another and burst out laughing.

"You look a fright," she giggled.

"Back at you."

She leaned up again and kissed him.

"What are we going to tell my folks?"

Rick slipped his hands around her waist and pulled her close. She searched his face, wondering what was going through his mind. Part of her wanted to run in terror, and part of her wanted to never leave his side again.

He brushed a wet strand of hair out of her eyes.

"First, we need to get these horses back and get home to your folks, who are probably worried sick. Then we'll get dried off, finish our meal, and then I'll head home. And maybe a week later, I will ask your father's permission to court you."

"Court me? Is this the Old West?"

"If you want it to be. I have no problem sweeping you off your feet and riding off into the sunset with you."

Serenity grinned at such a silly romantic notion, but her heart leaped inside her chest. He touched her face with his hand that was gentle despite its roughness.

"I want to do this right, Serenity. Right by you, your family, and God. I've been feeling myself being pulled to you ever since I got back, and I suppose deep down, that was what I was hoping for. I was just too scared, too ashamed, to admit that to you."

"It's okay," she said. "None of that matters now. We're in this together. Now let's get these horses back."

Rick took a hold of Crack Shot's lead line and then mounted Hillbilly. He pulled Serenity up behind him and tied Crack Shot's line to Hillbilly's saddle horn. Serenity hugged him tight, pressing her cheek against his wet back.

It's funny how life can change in just a few short moments.

The rain had diminished a bit and the lightning had thankfully moved off so the trip back was less eventful. They reached the barn and put the animals back in their stalls. Jasmine was pretty upset at being left alone but Serenity knew she was a tough gal who could take care of herself. When Crack Shot and Hillbilly were back inside, Jasmine brayed her happiness.

Rick fed and watered the horses as Serenity brushed Crack Shot's coat to help him calm down. She glanced over her shoulder and caught Rick smiling at her. She blushed and turned away.

Easy, girl. Take it slow.

She didn't have to remind herself. He said that he wanted to do right by her, and she was going to hold him to that. But that still didn't stop her from sneaking another glance behind her, admiring his broad shoulders and strong arms.

They locked the barn and headed back up to the house, but not before sharing one more quick kiss beneath the tree with Josh's initial carved into the bark. Serenity imagined him smiling down at them. Her heart was so full of happiness, she thought she might burst.

Patti and Greg were on the porch when they came up the hill.

"Oh, thank goodness!" Patti exclaimed, holding out two

towels. "We were worried sick!"

"Crack Shot ran off," Serenity said, running the towel over her neck and tussling her hair.

"Did you find him?" Greg asked.

"Yeah," Rick answered. "He was way out there but we brought him back."

"Well, get inside and get dried off," Patti ordered, opening the door and sweeping her hand inside. "Craziest Thanksgiving I can remember!"

Serenity caught Rick's eye. "That's for sure," she said with a sideways smile.

****

A week later, Rick showed up at the MacAlisters' house wearing a freshly-pressed buttoned-down shirt and holding a bouquet of flowers. Serenity answered the door and he announced that he would like to speak to Mr. and Mrs. MacAlister. When Patti and Greg came to the door, Rick said that he would like to speak with them alone. Serenity tried her best to act surprised and she excused herself, saying that she was going down to check on the horses.

As she tended to the animals and cleaned up around the barn, her stomach felt like it was filled with butterflies. She glanced up the hill, seeing only the roof of the house. What was being said in there?

What would Daddy do? Was Rick acting like a man or like a babbling, lovesick fool?

Serenity went to the door of the barn and looked out across the early December grass. She rested her arms against the bottom of the open door, folded her hands together, and closed her eyes.

"Lord, my life and my heart belong to You. I know I've messed up and I'm sure I'll mess up again. I need You to guide me and keep me from making stupid mistakes. Lord, I love Rick, I really do, and I feel that he really loves me. If this is Your plan for us, make our love grow strong, and let it be based on Your love for us, not just on romantic feelings or fear of loneliness or things like that. Let our love honor You."

She took a deep breath.

"If my parents agree, I'll take it as a sign that this is what You want for me, and I will be the best woman I can be for him. Amen."

The horses whinnied. Serenity smiled, thinking they were adding their own "amens" to her prayer, but then she heard footsteps coming down the path from the house. Fear pricked her heart for a moment, and then she told herself that she really meant what she had prayed. Her life, and her love, was in God's hands.

She tried to read Rick's face as he came to the barn door. His brow was furrowed and he seemed deep in thought.

He stood in front of her for a few moments, looking into her eyes but not saying anything.

Finally, Serenity held up her hands. "Well?"

Rick licked his lips. His face was very serious. "I've been in firefights with bullets whizzing over my head and mortars falling around me. Men screaming and dying. I can honestly say that talking to your folks just now was more terrifying than any of that."

Serenity's stomach dropped. "Why? What did they say?"

"Well, your father looked like he wanted to chop me up and throw me on the grill. Your mama looked like she might burst into tears at any moment, and I'm glad she didn't because I don't know what I would have done."

"So what did you say to them?"

"I told them how special y'all were to me, especially you, and how we would always share the painful memory of Josh's loss. But I also believe in the healing power of God's forgiveness, particularly in our need to forgive ourselves. The forgiveness your family has shown me has given me hope that one day I can truly forgive myself, and it also opened my eyes to your own journey down that same road. I told them flat-out that I have always had feelings for you, and since coming back here, they have grown and blossomed, and that you share the same feelings for me. We found ourselves pulled together like magnets, searching for the hope to love without being heartbroken, and also for the forgiveness that we can help each other find. And then I asked the question, looking at your father but really talking to both of them: would I have their blessing to court you in keeping with godly and moral conduct?"

Serenity's palms were sweating. "What was their answer?"

Rick exhaled and smiled. "They said they would absolutely bless our courtship. Your mama said she would be 'tickled pink and rolled in sprinkles.'"

Serenity squealed and threw her arms around his neck. "Oh Rick, I'm so happy!"

Rick gave her a squeeze, then held her at arm's length. "Your father agreed as well, but I think I'm going to have to do a little work to win him over. I was hardly a model boyfriend before and a daughter is every father's treasure. He took me out back and gave me a stern talking–to. But I'm determined not to give him any reason to question my character. I mean it, Serenity. I'm going to treat you right, as a godly woman, our Heavenly Father's treasure."

Tears sparkled in Serenity's eyes. She leaned forward and gave him a gentle kiss.

"I love you, Rick Stevens."

"I love you too, Serenity Hope." He took her hand. "Come on, your folks would like to talk to both of us together."

Serenity threaded her fingers in his. She couldn't wipe the smile off her face even if she tried. Hand in hand, they walked up the hill toward the house that would always be home.

EPILOGUE

SERENITY SQUINTED in the bright June sunshine, turning her head so the brim of her hat shielded her eyes. She pulled the reins to the left and Jasmine responded to her command. The horse walked over to the fence where a group of people were gathered at the gate. Rick was telling a story and everyone was laughing.

He turned and smiled at her when she rode up.

"Miss Serenity," he said, tipping his hat and giving her a wink.

"Mr. Rick," she replied with a smile that was just a little too sweet to be purely professional. She didn't care if the others noticed.

Rick stepped back with a flourish. "They're all yours."

"Thank you." She sat up on her horse, looking at the eager faces in front of her. Most of them were middle-aged with a few seniors mixed in. They all looked like they came from city money but she could see the sparkle of adventure in their eyes.

"Howdy, folks!" she announced loudly. Her voice was strong

and well–rehearsed by now.

"Howdy!" the group replied.

"Welcome to Horton Ranch, Jonesburg edition. You've already met Rick Stevens. My name is Serenity MacAlister."

Her eyes flashed.

"Now, are y'all ready to have some fun?"

The End

A WORD FROM MICHAEL

I hope you liked this book. It was fun to write and there are more on the way. I would greatly appreciate it if you would leave a review on Amazon, Goodreads, social media, and anywhere you might tell everyone how you felt about *Serenity Hope*. Even if you didn't like it, I'd still want you to let folks know. And if you want to let me know what you thought or just want to say "Howdy," you can send me an email at michaelwinstellbooks@gmail.com and I'll get back to you lickety-split.

God bless and happy trails!

Coming Soon!

CHASTITY GRACE

He Calls Me by Name – Book 2

Coming Soon!

CHARITY JOY

He Calls Me by Name – Book 3

MICHAEL WINSTELL lives in north Georgia.

You can find him online at:

www.michaelwinstell.com

www.facebook.com/michaelwinstell

65014902R00175

Made in the USA
Middletown, DE
24 February 2018